The Formation of Us

Labels & Lace

YD La Mar

Acknowledgments

To my wonderful husband, who never bats an eye when I come up with crazy ideas, but instead just adds to it, making my stories come alive. My children, who tell me every day that they are proud of me.

To my beta readers. You guys are the real MVP. Thank you for sticking with me through the initial phases of my writing journey. All of your feedback has inspired me to better myself and my writing ability. Anita, Alex, Dana, Vicky, Maria, **Terri**, **Tree**, Beth, Shaddy, **Kylie**, Gloria, Sasha, and **everyone** who responded to my beta request in the dark group, and everyone else who beta read, thank you for bouncing ideas with me.

To all my readers, thank you for giving me the chance. I hope I can continue to make you guys proud.

Names

Matunaagd Big Crow

Atsuko Kobayashi

Mohd Akmal Bin Aqli

Veronica "Vero" Hernandez

Travis Boyd

Miss Megan Miller

Tricia Smith

Alfonso Torres

Mortimer "Morty" Archambault

Translations

¿Qué carajo tu putas creen estas haciendo? : What the fuck do you bitches think you're doing?

Makan : Eat

Na-ahks' : The term for both grandfather and grandmother in Blackfoot

Blurb

Banished from the reservation before the fires even died
down,
my guilt and shadows followed me.
My hands stained in blood, a friendly soul helped me get
back on my feet.
Through the lens of a friend's camera, my eyes catch the most
beautiful woman I've ever seen.
She wasn't the kind of woman who let me admire her from
afar.
Her confidence pulled me in, her strength helped break me
out of my shell.
A slice of heaven I probably didn't deserve.
When the dark stain on my soul rears its ugly head, will she
be strong enough to remain by my side? Or will she leave it
all behind like ashes in the wind?

Courtesy Warning: This book may contain triggers for some. Triggers include but not limited to: domestic violence, violence, non con/dub con.

*** This book may contain authentic speech used by the different nationalities/ethnicities represented in this book. Some grammar usage was purposely done with broken English to continue to allow the story to flow authentically. ***

Prologue

MATUNAAGD

I can smell it before I get there. It's a scent that has burned itself into my very soul, accompanied by the feeling of dread in the pit of my stomach. *No.*

The tribe sent me to college to get a further education that would help the Casino. Software engineering was what I chose to go for. It's been over four years. Four years of not being able to watch over my mother when my father gets in these moods.

Our home on the reservation looks like a log cabin. The sight of it is homey, the feel of it is tense. A tension that prickles your spine every time you walk into it.

Walking up to the front now, I see the door is barely hanging on the hinges. *Shit.* My heart is beating out of its chest, a rhythm like war drums, as my mind is running through all the worst-case scenarios. I'm actually hoping that someone tried to rob the house and my parents are out because the other possibility makes my blood run cold. My skull starts to feel tighter and tighter the more my memories flit through my mind.

"Are you fucking cheating on me again, woman? I knew it!" With each syllable that comes out of his mouth, the scent of whiskey becomes stronger and stronger. His words start to slur together at the end.

"No, no... I was out getting some food." The way her voice shakes, the sound of her vulnerability, makes me ball up my fists. When Dad gets like this, I never know what to expect.

"You and your lies! I know you've been whoring around! Always trying to get away from me!" His hands grab at his hair and pull it out in frustration. "What's wrong with me, huh? Am I not enough for you or something? I see the way the other men look at you!" His voice raises in octaves with every inhale he takes. I don't even think he realizes his current state. His eyes are bloodshot, his nostrils flaring like a primal beast that's scented its prey.

"It's not like that. I haven't done anything wrong." Her voice is so soft that the sound of the slap against her cheek is sharp and makes my teeth grind. Thwack! I jump in front of my mother and shove him off her, out of instinct. The hairs on the back of my neck standing on edge in challenge. I've had enough of this! How long can my mother be his punching bag?!

I don't see the backhand until it's too late, the sharp pain making me feel like my skin is about to rip off my face. The sting and the warmth of the blood that starts to slowly dribble out the edge of my mouth, a contrast to how cold I feel inside. How can I share blood ties with this beast before me?

"Don't talk back to me. She's mine to discipline. She's only mine. She has no right to whore herself out!" The sound of my mother's sobs sears into my ears like a scar that will never heal. Each hiccup creates a fresh, jagged wound on my soul. I need to protect her.

Running through the front door, my feet grind to a halt at what I find. My heart stutters in an off rhythm, making my chest hurt.

The floor is flooded in crimson. The color is drowning out everything else around me. My mother lies face down like she's resting while my father's open-eyed stoic expression stares at me, almost *accusing* me of not being here to stop his uncontrollable transgressions. Almost as if the beast inside of him took over, and it was *my* fault I wasn't there to challenge him.

The anger I've just only learned to control now spikes to infernal levels. My mind feels tight, my throat is closed, and I can't even roar in anger. I can feel myself bare my teeth and grind down in frustration and pain. It was bound to happen. I knew it. *I knew it!* Why did I let the damn reservation convince me to leave? Damn it all!

Where are they when I need them? Did no one hear the gunshots? There's no other person here to stare into the lifeless eyes that stare back at me...but ME.

I feel like Atlas, with the weight of the world on my shoulders, about to crumble with everything that's thrown at me. My shoulders physically do fall as my knees hit the ground in defeat, slipping on the blood beneath me. Despite the lifeless corpses still within my view, the weight hasn't been removed from my shoulders. I feel betrayed. I feel like a child left out to the elements to die and wither as I watch the downfall of my family lying here in a pool of blood.

The blood that seeps into my pants is cool. How long have they been here like this? The beast within me howls in anguish and refuses to let the reservation take the home I once called mine. The reservation that has brought no saviors to the horrors inside here. No, there will be no more of this. They will remember the pain and suffering they have caused during my absence. The *absence* they created. It will all fall down to their feet, branding them as this moment has branded me.

GUILTY.

My mind is a haze as my body moves through some sort of muscle memory, leading me to the decisions my mind has not yet made. It zones out as I walk back and forth, back and forth, performing movements my mind's eye cannot see.

Dousing my emotions, dousing everything. A send off. My mother to the heavens and my father, the very pits of hell. I almost don't even recognize my own body's movements at this point. Only bits and pieces come back to me as I return to the log cabin one last time.

Standing out in the front, I feel blank. I feel numb...the nothingness of what was left to me. I *am nothing* now. With a flick of my wrist, it is done. The heat on my face brings back only a sliver of sensation to my skin, reminding me of reality, reminding me of the life that still flows through my veins. The glow surrounding me, lighting up what was kept in the dark. *It should have never been kept in the dark.*

As the flames devour the log cabin I once called home with a roar, I turn slowly to walk back to my car and drive towards the exit out of the reservation, never looking back or even glancing at the rear-view mirror.

Who I was is now gone. The betrayal of the reservation is sitting heavy in my heart. It's time I created something new from the ashes of the past.

———

I know I shouldn't be doing this after what happened with my parents. It's been a couple of weeks, but fuck, starting over was harder than I thought. My pride was what carried me over the reservations ground. But now? Where do I go from here? Where the hell do I start?

I ended up at a damn bar of all places, drinking light beer, but enough of it that I'm getting tipsy. Shit, I need to stop while I'm ahead.

My ears pick up on a masculine voice saying, "Bitch, just wait until we get home. Don't fucking give me lip out here if you know what's good for you. Just do as you're told!" Fucking hell, I can't seem to get away from bastards like my father.

I don't know what possesses me, but I follow the couple out of the bar. It's already dark outside, with other drunks hanging around, so my presence is easily hidden.

They must have parked pretty far because we've been walking for a while.

My head snaps to the woman when I see her jerky move-ments from struggling to run away from her husband towards an alleyway. What the fuck just happened? Fresh thoughts of my mother come back to me and how I never knew if she ever ran or tried to get away. I never knew how hard she fought.

The husband is growling like an enraged beast, with exple-tives spilling out of his mouth like vomit. *Just like my damn father.*

My eyes are seeing red as I catch up to him and slam him into the wall, the sound of his skull hitting the concrete making me excited to catch my prey. I'm going to make sure he never hurts another person again, especially a woman.

My fists, rage and feeling of missed justice start to intermix, creating a heady potion to my senses. I barely feel anything but my fist hitting something solid again and again. My eyes catch a piece of broken glass beside me and with quick move-ments, I shove the pointy end in and out, left and right. There's something wet and warm on my face, but I don't think I've been crying. I'm too excited and angry to cry. I've cried out all my tears already after my mother was killed. No, Father will never put his hands on her again.

When I finally realize the gentleman isn't making any moves to fight back, my hands slow down and my chest continues to heave in and out until my vision clears up.

The rank smell of the alleyway finally seeping into my nostrils over the metallic smell of blood. Something inside my palms starts to sting and I realize I've been tightly holding onto the shard of glass with a death grip. How did it even get there?

My head lifts up when a shadow looms over me. It looks like a woman, but the drinks I've had are not making me see too clearly. The rage that's leaving my system is not making me see what I should.

"I should be mad, but I'm not." The longer I stare, the more I can see her tear-streaked face with mascara running down the same path, surrounded by a halo of dark brown hair. My mother's face on the floor of our cabin flits through my mind and disappears when the woman places a gentle hand on my shoulder.

"Thank you for saving me. I didn't know how I would be able to get away. I didn't have a way out at all." She comes onto her knees next to me and moves her palm over one of my bloodstained fists, reminding me to let go of the glass.

"I'll tell them there was an altercation with a stranger and he got away. I'll describe him as someone else. Is there anything I can do to help you? You need to get out of here."

I can't believe what I'm hearing. Is this a sign? It has to be. I think...I think I just killed a man. The Queen song runs through my head at that moment, and I almost laugh. What the hell is wrong with me? Has my father's darkness tainted our bloodline? This is exactly why I needed to get away from the reservation. I couldn't be his son. I needed to break away from it all.

How can she help me? I need a damn job. I don't know where to go from here. Only a short time off the reservation and I'm already in a load of shit.

"I need to find work. I need to get on my feet."

"What do you do? I may be able to call up some friends."

I do chuckle then because we're having this damn conversation right by a dead corpse. What the hell is wrong with my life? How does it keep going from shit to shittier?

"Software engineering."

"I might actually be able to help you with that. I know someone who's been looking for more employees. He's not the best guy around, but it's honest work."

Chapter One

MATUNAAGD

She keeps calling me over. I know what she wants, and it isn't IT help with her computer modem. She's given me such good reviews that the higher-ups keep putting me with her open cases. Every time I get there it's because of something trivial, for instance not plugging the power cord in.

Pulling up the company car to her neighborhood, I almost feel a sense of dread. It's always like this between us. The sad part about it is, I both enjoy it and hate it to my very core. She wants to brand herself inside of me, that's what she truly hopes to accomplish. Like the taming of the wild mustang, the domestication of a wild wolf. The more I fight, the more she latches on, trying to break me.

The houses in this neighborhood look like the typical suburban town, like the ones you see in Hollywood movies. Surrounded by mostly light-skinned faces, they watch you like a predator just entered their midst. All the homes have well-manicured lawns that almost make you scared of what's on the inside because *nothing* is this perfect. No one is this perfect. Life has thrown enough shit in my face to show me this. The veil of this neighborhood doesn't fool me.

When I pull up the car to her pristine concrete driveway and put the car in park, I throw my head back against the headrest. The firm pressure against my head grounding me. I crack my head left and right, rolling it against the headrest before letting out a loud sigh.

Shit, let's get this over with then.

Grabbing my bag of tools, I straighten my clothes as I walk towards the front door, ready with a false smile.

She opens it before I even have the chance to ring the doorbell. Standing in the doorway wearing a black silk robe with her red hair tied up in a messy knot on top of her head. To a passerby, it would just look like a woman who's comfortable at home. To me, I know the truth. I can see through her tactics.

Miss Miller is a beast on the prowl. A huntress. Or what most people call a cougar.

"What seems to be the problem today, Miss Miller?" We do this song and dance every time. The smile that graces her face makes me want to flinch back but I keep my body standing still until I'm invited in. She has plans. She always does.

She grabs the front of my shirt and pulls me in with all her strength, making sure to shut and lock the front door behind us. I drop my bag onto the ground, knowing that I won't get a word in until she allows me to.

See, Miss Miller has a specific appetite. An appetite to *dominate.*

She drags me into her bedroom, turns me around and throws me down on my back, quickly taking off my work boots and pants. The adeptness of her fingers is borderline admirable because she does it without taking her sharp green eyes off me; commanding me to submit with a trained look. Miss Miller controls the situation as my mind starts to zone out.

It's been five years since leaving the reservation, though on my bad days it feels like just yesterday.

Driving towards the direction of the city, I'm almost off the reservation grounds when a few of the men stop me. Some of the people nearby have soot on their faces. Everyone around me has a look of grim determination.

I'm numb to it all.

When a crime is committed on the reservation, the tribe handles their own. Not that their decision matters anyway, because I'm getting out of this place one way or another. I no longer wish to be associated with a people that have essentially left my family in a pool of blood long enough for it to cool.

They banished me off the grounds despite still having grandparents there. I turned my back on them as well, head held high, the way they so easily turned their backs on me.

I gulp when Miss Miller climbs over my body to straddle my naked hips, bringing me back to the present. She opens her robe, revealing she's only wearing a corset that covers her waist. I inwardly groan because I hate that she corners me like this, but fuck if I don't sometimes love the shit she does to my dick. The thing has a mind of its own and is a bad judge of character.

She removes the hair tie I have in place, spilling my long black hair onto the sheets beneath us right before she grabs it and tilts my head to the side so she can lick up the cord of my neck, branding me. I shouldn't be letting her do this to me. It freaked me out the first time two years ago, especially because I was a damn virgin. The only short reprieve I got from her was during my month-long vacation from work. I was able to avoid her for another week after that.

I couldn't beat this woman off me with a stick, not that I would. I'm not that kind of guy. Especially after growing up with a father like mine. But some days my fingers itch to throw her body against the wall and watch it slide down with streaks of blood, just to end the misery she puts me in. The guilt over thinking that way sobers me. *I am not my father.*

Her teeth bite down over my right pec almost hard enough to break the skin before she licks it and bites again. I can handle her for the most part, but when she's in a mood like this, I wish I could do more than just 'handle' her.

Closing my eyes, trying to remove my thoughts away from the moment, I hiss in pain when she slaps my dick like she's pissed that it came here to her house like she asked it to.

A few more hard slaps and I'm about to grab her wrist when she swallows my entire dick whole into her warm, wet mouth. Fuck!

Miss Miller is the horniest forty-five-year-old woman I've ever known. It doesn't say much since I've only been with a few girls after she took what didn't belong to her. Women who were willing to fuck me because I seem like a novelty to them. They randomly propositioned me, and I was out of my mind enough to agree. I'm not great with my dating game, but I forcefully put myself out there in hopes of it helping me to remove myself from her clawed grip. But damn if she doesn't weave a tight web around me.

When her mouth starts to suction harder and her nails dig into my balls, I can't help but tense up, making her moan loudly over my straining cock. Her tongue running across the tip of the head, playing with it seductively makes me want to groan, but I swallow it back down. I'm giving her too much already. Right when I think I can't take her abuse on my dick anymore, she removes her mouth with a nip just behind the crown of the head and climbs me like a fucking fallen tree.

She spears herself with my cock and starts to circle her clit with her hands. She never lets me move. She uses me like a damn blow-up doll, a dead piece of flesh with a hard cock. The degradation is what kills me inside each and every time.

She fucks me harder and harder like she's riding a damn bull and soon enough I feel her pussy clenching my dick like it's her mouth all over again. I'm so close, but so far from my climax, it messes with my mind.

My logical brain reminds me how fucked up this whole thing is. When she's done finding pleasure, she fucking leaves me there to clean myself up, not even letting me get my own release. Sometimes when she's not looking, I let my hand quickly stroke myself against the skin of my shaft to release the pressure in the restroom while I'm 'allowed to clean up'.

It seems today is one of those days.

Once the incident that shall not be named is put behind us, I go back to the living room to pick up the bag I dropped on the way in. Today, Miss Miller thought cutting straight through the Cat 5 cable with a fucking knife will bring me to her faster. I sigh as I continue to keep my thoughts to myself, quickly remedying the problem.

I give her my mumbled goodbyes without looking her in the eyes before hightailing it out of there. When my face feels the fresh air outside, I let out another harsh breath. This woman is going to kill me. I need to do something.

When I drive through the quaint suburban town, some of the neighbors who have come out look at me with suspicion. It doesn't matter if I'm in a company car or not. People who look like me do not usually tread around these parts. Darker skin, long black hair tied back, my cheekbones and dark eyes give away my heritage. The tattoos that peek out don't help out either, I'm sure.

Another sigh of relief comes out of me when I finally exit the town and head back to headquarters.

Walking past a couple of the co-workers, I wave at them with a false smile pretending it's just a normal day and I didn't just have a woman essentially force me into a compromised position.

Is this what I'm going to be doing for the rest of my days? I can't handle any more Miss Millers in this line of work. Thank goodness there's only been one. My soul would be sucked out and leave me just a shell of a person.

"Hey Mat, did you run into any problems with the Miller call?" Shit, if only he knew. Akmal is the only guy I allow to call me Mat, since he's probably my only close friend. Matunaagd: 'He who fights'; some days I still feel like I didn't fight enough to keep my mother alive. Coming back from Miss Miller's house, I feel like I didn't fight enough to keep her away from me.

"Nah, it was an easy fix." Akmal and I have become close since we started working at the company at the same time. He was the friendliest guy there at orientation, making it easy for me to get along with him. He's Malaysian, standing at five-feet-seven inches, his skin only a shade or two lighter than mine. We could almost pass as brothers if it wasn't for my six-feet-two inch height and broader build. In fact, many of our co-workers call him the pocket version of me, much to his dismay, since we're always hanging out together.

"If Tricia were here, you know she would have diverted the case to someone else. She knows how much you don't like going over there."

"Yeah, thank goodness for small blessings. But she wasn't here today so I had to take care of it."

"It's been pretty slow today for me. You want to go get lunch and get out of here?"

"Yeah, that actually sounds really good." I need more fresh air to get the feeling of Miss Miller out of me.

We both clock out together and Akmal decides he'll drive us down the street today to the sandwich shop we usually frequent, Sammi's Sandwiches.

Sitting on their metal chairs outside, I think about my time working at the company. There really isn't much room for advancement. Morty's been kind enough to take me in after a call made on my behalf. Just Techs is a joke under the guise of a technical support company. We do perform tech support, but I swear there's something shady happening in the background I'm unaware of. To be honest, I really don't care. It's dragging my life and soul down at this point. That thought alone makes me feel like I'm strapped to a damn ball and chain. The thought of being forever trapped in the vicious cycle with Miss Miller makes me want to choke on my own vomit.

"Hey Akmal, have you ever thought about doing something else?"

Akmal is chewing his turkey sandwich thoughtfully before he responds. "I don't know. I guess not. I mean, I have hobbies I do on the side. Why what's up?"

What's up? I feel like my soul wants to roam, but it doesn't have a path or direction. A yearning without a destination. A lone wolf with no actual territory to call his own.

"I don't know man." I truly don't.

Our waitress comes by right as I'm just about to finish up my sandwich, shoving the last bite into my mouth.

"How was it? Was there anything else I can get you?"

I'm just swallowing my last bite when I realize she's staring at me. Is there something on my face? I try to discreetly wipe my mouth with a napkin and look away, hoping to cover the flush on my cheeks. This is pretty awkward. Why is she leaning towards me like that? I can see her just fine where she's standing. Maybe she has a sight problem or something and needs to lean in closer.

"Oh yes, I'd love a dessert to go, please." She's not even hearing Akmal, who's literally talking to her shoulder. She's just staring at me. Sheesh. I think it's time to go.

Scooting my chair back, I get up and put my cash on the table. Akmal, looking put out by her non-response, does the same.

He tries to give her a polite smile on the way out, but she continues to stare at me with a smile of her own and blinks one eyelid. Why is she winking like that? This situation makes me feel a bit strange and uncomfortable. I turn to head back to the car, with Akmal right behind me.

We head back to work and our regional manager, Morty, is informing the team that we'll be getting a new guy tomorrow.

I don't feel anything about it either way. I still don't know what I should be doing with my life, but I can't help but feel like my spirit is being pulled somewhere. Somewhere that's not here at Just Techs.

Chapter Two

MAT

"Alright guys, gather around. This here is Travis Boyd; he's going to be joining our team as of today. I want you guys to show him the ropes and start taking him out on some of your cases so he can see how you guys do things in the field." Despite his speech, I've never once seen Morty go out or take anyone out in the field since I've started working here. He's always hiding in his office until the day is done. What the hell does he do in there?

"Hey Mat, I was thinking about what we were talking about the other day." Morty's voice is droning on in the background as Akmal speaks in low tones next to me.

"What's that?"

"I've always been into photography. Taking pictures as a hobby and such. I've done some freelance work but maybe I should see if I can do more with it?"

"You're farther than I am. I haven't come up with jack shit. Let me know how it goes, I'll support you, man."

"I'll support you too." I didn't even realize Tricia was standing next to us, listening to our conversation.

"Gentleman and ladies, please pay attention." Akmal and I share a sheepish glance before we stare at Morty, giving him our utmost attention.

"Alright, since you think you don't need to hear this, Travis will be following you today, Aqli." Akmal makes a face at me because he hates it when the boss says his name like that, like he's crap under his shoe.

"Yes, boss." Akmal is right. I need to find ways to use my skillset elsewhere. I need to get out of this company and away from people like Morty.

I was able to avoid Miss Miller today, thanks to Tricia handling the calls coming in. The thought of that woman puts me on pins and needles, which only adds to the way I feel about this job. The day went by smoothly without that extra case to handle.

Driving home, I feel a sense of relief wash over me. Walking through the front door of my apartment, a calm settles over my entire being. *Home sweet home.* Located on the lower level, not too far from the city, the apartment is big enough for a guy like me.

Two bedrooms, a kitchen and a bathroom. Nice and simple. Thinking of the bathroom, I start stripping down out of my uniform and tossing the clothes into the dirty hamper before stepping inside for a hot shower. The cool tile beneath my feet reinvigorates me. My hair's grown out halfway down my back, the feeling of the ends sliding against my skin. I can't seem to bring myself to cut it just yet. Am I holding onto a past that I should let go of? Thoughts of my parents drift back into my mind, and much too soon, the images are tainted in a red haze.

I punch the tile wall with a *thwack*, the throbbing in my knuckles grounding me back into the present. I'm tired of the way they still haunt me; the way my guilt still shrouds me. My hand grabs the soap, ignoring the sting, and starts to lather my upper body across the scattering of multiple colorful tattoos I've collected over time. Wanting the pain of the needle to numb the ones on the inside when it washes over me like a tidal wave.

It's probably about that time again, the time to get fresh ink. As I continue to lather and wash my hair, I start to wonder if I should just cut it all off and start over, really let the past go. *I should.*

The warmth of the shower leaves me too quickly once I'm done and toss on some boxers and shorts. Being a bachelor means I have a lot of pre-made meals in the fridge, but it suits me just fine.

Plopping myself down on the chair by my kitchen table, I open up my laptop that's been sitting there. Deciding to unwind with a little gaming, I open up the chat server while I eat my reheated meal. Chewing a few bites, I realize this is not one of my favorite Hungry Man microwave meals. I'll have to remember to never buy it again.

Akmal is already online with a few of the other guys we've grown to know from teaming up in the game. I don't even remember how I came up with my screenname tinfoilhat, but I just stuck with it. Akmal's screen name still makes me chuckle no matter how many times I've seen it. His ode to wishing he was taller.

Shaquille.oatmeal : Hey, I got this photography gig next month at a car show.

PaniniHead : @ ima.robot, are you logging into play tonight?

Tinfoilhat : Sweet, I bet you'll kill it.

Avocadorable : Congrats!

Shaquille.oatmeal : I'm so nervous, man. I've never shot such a big crowd or event before, mostly individual or family portraits. My hands are getting sweaty just thinking about it.

Ima.robot : Yeah, let me finish up my food and I'll login real quick.

Tinfoilhat : I'm sure you'll be fine. You got talent, that's why they requested you.

Avocadorable : He's right, you'll do great.

Shaquille.oatmeal : Yeah, I guess you're right.

We continue the night chatting about stupid stuff and play some first-person shooter games until the crew starts disconnecting to end their night one at a time. It's the best way to unwind at the end of the day. Some nights we switch it up with other MMO games.

Shutting off my laptop, I walk myself to bed to lay down. The softness of the comforter envelops me in coolness before absorbing the warmth from my skin. Running my hand through my hair, I decide I *will* cut it to change things up. My hand runs across my chest and I think of what other kind of artwork I should get. Both of my pecs are completely covered, as well as one full sleeve on my left and three-quarter sleeve on my right.

My right hand grazes across my abs, and I can feel my dick twitching in response. I guess I could cover this area. My mind starts to wander as my hand reaches inside my shorts to grab my semi-hard dick and starts slowly stroking.

Shit, don't think about Miss Miller. Don't think about Miss Miller. My dick starts to soften at the mental image of her face, and I have to physically shake my head and think of something else. The shadow of a woman enters my mind. I'd want her smaller than me. I'd want her to be the opposite of me in general because I can barely deal with myself on normal days. I can't see her face, but I can see her body just fine. The contrast of her skin against mine makes a heady potion for me. Like a forbidden flower that I crave to pluck and sully.

She's sensual. Her long black tresses flowing over her delicate shoulders make me want to run my hands through it to see if it's really as silky as it looks.

My dick starts to harden as my mind plays images of the mysterious woman disrobing, her dark perky nipples making my mouth water. Each breast is just more than a handful. Gripping my cock harder, I continue the slow and steady rhythm I have going as my mind reveals her soft pink lips slightly parting.

My mind is running through all the different scenarios we would have together. Her face is still shrouded in darkness, but her smile, my god, her smile lights up my fucking life. It feeds my soul with something addictive. Her full lips making promises I'm only given a glimpse to. A man like me doesn't deserve it, but fuck if I don't want to steal it.

I visualize her in a swimsuit; I visualize her in office wear with her creamy breasts overflowing and spilling out her unbuttoned white top that does nothing to hide the red bra she has underneath. She bites her bottom lip gently with her teeth and she begs so sweetly with just a look. Each scenario my mind pictures with her, is a scenario with me dominating her. The yearning to cover her with my body, to control everything that's happening between us. The magic that I have to weave for her to be under my spell. And she would love me being selfish, taking everything from her.

When my illusion woman bends over a desk and spreads her round ass cheeks to offer herself to me, my sack tightens. My other hand roughly brings down my shorts, exposing my cock to the air as I pull back the skin of my dick with a firm grip and cum all over my abs with a groan. It takes a moment for me to slow my breathing and come back down to reality.

Damn, now I got to clean up again.

Chapter Three

MAT

My muscles burn with every stride I take. The pounding of my feet on the pavement, the heat rising up from what the sun has baked all day. On the days my demons take over too much of my mind, I run. As swift as the wolves in the forest, I hope to outrun the memories and feelings of guilt that drown me when I'm in too deep. I need to get lost in the motion, the wind in my face, the smell of earth around me.

My chosen path is a decent sized park nearby. Sweat drips down my face, almost making it to my eye, and I wipe it off with the back of my forearm. It glides as it mixes with the sweat that's already accumulated there as well. It's a good seventy-seven degrees Fahrenheit today, but the brutal pace I'm setting for myself is making me sweat buckets. Taking off my shirt, I wipe my whole head down and tuck it in the back pocket of my shorts.

Just two more rounds. My calves and thighs are burning, but I need the pain. I need to ground myself back to the present, back to sanity.

Finishing up my run at the far end of the park, the walk back to the apartment is my cooldown. I only brought one bottle of water with me, so I had to pace my drinking. Three quarters for the run and a quarter for the end. Finishing it off while I stand in front of my building, I go to toss the bottle in the trash can when I hear a gasp from behind me.

Turning around, one of the older ladies in my apartment building is shielding the eyes of what looks to be her teenage granddaughter. I feel my face flush as I mumble an apology before grabbing my shirt from the back and putting it back on. I'm sure she's offended by the tattoos on my back and wouldn't want her granddaughter to get ideas.

I leave the scene as quickly as I can, walking towards my apartment door. Sticking my keys into the lock, I hear something behind me. Turning to see what it is, I see a young woman who looks to be in her mid-twenties. She has a weird expression on her face.

"Is everything okay?"

She clears her throat and her voice sounds a little shaky. Maybe there's something going around?

"Um, yes. Sorry about that. I was just walking to my apartment and got distracted. You must be one of my neighbors?"

There's been an empty apartment a couple of doors down. She must be the one moving in since I don't recognize her.

"Yeah, I live in 145. You must be moving into 149? It's been empty for a while." She giggles and starts to twirl her brown hair. I'm still trying to figure out what she's laughing about when she responds.

"Yea, that's me. 149. I'm Emily, by the way."

"Mat." There's an awkward silence that follows, and I think I'm wearing out my hello, so I try to make a quick getaway.

"I need to, uh, hit the showers. It was nice meeting you." Not waiting for her to answer, I shut the door right after I walk inside. I'm not great with these pleasantries and I'm sweaty as hell. She was probably clearing her throat because I smell funky.

Stripping out of wet clothes is disgusting, but the ice-cold shower is just what I need after a hard run, like the one I just finished. Feels good to get clean and cool down. I probably shouldn't wash my hair this often, but it was sweat drenched as well. Quickly finishing up, I get out and grab the towel on the shower door.

Not bothering to put on any clothes yet, I walk around the apartment to help air dry my hair. I really should start cooking instead of eating these microwave meals, to be honest. It probably affects my workouts. Akmal and I have a guys' night tonight on my couch to catch some old Star Wars movies on the flat screen. We've both seen it already, but we still enjoy kicking it and drinking a couple of light beers.

Walking back to my bathroom, I braid my hair in front of the mirror. Staring at the empty expanse on my abs, I'm glad I made that appointment at the tattoo shop. Getting dressed in a loose t-shirt and jeans, I grab the images I printed off this morning from the printer tray.

Exiting the door, I don't see Emily or any of the other neighbors on my way to the apartment parking lot. The tattoo shop is about a twenty-minute drive from my home. Letting down the front windows of the car, I bask in the cool breeze that comes in on the drive there.

The ink shop is pretty empty today when I walk in. Good, the less people the better. I'm not the greatest in big and boisterous crowds. This shop is known for groups of rowdy drunk kids coming through a time or two since it's located not too far from a local college.

"Hey! Good to see you again. What are we going to be getting done today?"

"Hey, Chris! I'm thinking about something to cover the expanse of my stomach."

"Alright. Do you have a picture in mind already or do you need me to sketch something up?"

"Nah, I know exactly what I have in mind." I proceed to tell him the details and show him some of the images I printed off Pinterest this morning.

He takes a few moments to trace the picture for a stencil as I hang out in the lobby and set up my playlist on my phone.

Once he's done, Chris calls me to the back and preps his station as one of his co-workers takes over the front desk. Laying back, I make sure to put on my earphones as Chris gets to work. The sound of Zakk Wylde's voice and guitar drifts into my ear as I almost doze off, listening to Black Label Society. The sting of the needle against my skin creates an ache I enjoy, one I sometimes find myself craving more of.

My mind drifts back to Miss Miller and my mood sours. Is it her? Has she tainted me mentally that I now need this pain to feel something pleasurable? I can't even call what she gives me pleasurable when it's all said and done. The feeling of her against my skin lingers after the act, making me want to scrub my skin raw with stone. The humiliation and the degradation makes me want to claw my eyes out.

I must be tensing up because Chris taps me a few times, reminding me to relax. Chris is my go-to tattoo artist. He's great at what he does and he's efficient. Thanks to Miss Miller, my pain threshold is higher than it ever was. Chris and I agreed to power through an eight-hour session today, finishing it up at the next appointment.

He taps me again in a different pattern, letting me know we're done and I bring myself to the mirror. The majority of it is there. A Native American wolf baring his teeth in challenge with a crow overhead, his wingspan opened wide and traveling along under my pecs. I decided to go with just black ink to signify the past, the death, and rebirth.

"Hey, thanks, man. I'll see you at the next appointment."

"Yeah, see you next month." I slide him a hundred dollar bill as a tip before turning to leave his station.

Exiting the doors, I walk towards my Honda Civic sedan. My stomach stings a bit when I reach forward to start the ignition but I revel in the burn. I hope Akmal doesn't expect me to walk him to the door tonight after I sit my ass on the couch with a nice ice-cold beer.

The drive home felt longer than the drive there, probably because my mind kept thinking about the stinging from my sitting position. Once I got out of the car after parking, I let out a breath. Not really paying attention to my surroundings and moving on muscle memory to my door, I hear someone clear their throat behind me a few times as I'm inserting my key.

Turning around, I see Emily and she looks straight into my eyes. She must have something to say.

"Is everything okay?"

"Yea, I just wanted to say hi. You know, since we're crossing paths and all." Her laugh sounds a little strange, but maybe that's how she normally laughs and I just don't know it. I mean, I've just met the girl.

"Oh, okay. Well, hi."

She laughs again before saying hi once more and I'm saved from any further awkward conversation when Akmal walks up behind me and slaps me on the back in greeting.

"What's up, man? I take it your appointment went well?" Akmal's got a small six-pack of beer in his hand as I open the door and let us in. I nod my head to him and tip my head up to Emily for a goodbye before I shut the door and lock it. What a weird woman. Maybe she's lonely and doesn't have anyone to talk to. I think there's an animal shelter not too far away from here. Maybe she needs to get a dog or something.

Akmal automatically puts the cold ones in the fridge. He comes over so often, I don't have to tell him to make himself at home. Grabbing a beer, I head to the couch and relax, kicking off my boots.

Akmal does the same and we're browsing Netflix, seeing what new releases pop up. Akmal usually only chugs down two drinks max because of his culture, or so he's told me. He's not even supposed to be drinking at all but he's a little bit of a rule-breaker in his family. He's informed me that in Malaysia, they are much stricter and since he's not there, he's much laxer about it.

We ended up deciding on a Marvel remake instead of Star Wars and keep the volume at a medium. We tend to do our talking during the movie anyway since we can't talk as much as we would like at work without people eavesdropping on our conversation.

"How's your family doing?"

Akmal gulps his drink before letting out a burp to the side. "Ah, they're alright. Same, same. Two of my sisters are still living with my parents, of course. My middle sister is going to university now, so she spends most of her time there and has a little house near campus to make attending her classes easier. My parents are still bugging me about finding a woman to marry so they can have a million grandkids to spoil."

I chuckle because I've met his parents a few times. Despite how friendly they are, they scare me. I've cut back my visits because every time I'm over there, they try to get me to marry their oldest daughter. It's nerve-wracking. I'm not good with big crowds and conversation to begin with, but I don't want them to think I don't appreciate their hospitality.

"Mat! Come in, Come in. Akmal, you don't visit us enough." The friendliness of Akmal's family threw me for a loop the first time I met them. Now it's become more anticipated. Once we both enter, Akmal's mother looks behind us and frowns.

"Akmal, why didn't you bring anyone, huh? You need to find someone so I can have grandchildren while I'm still alive." I stifle a laugh as Akmal groans through her tirade. It's the same conversation every time we see her.

His parents start pushing both of us towards the floor to join in on their lunch. The house smells amazing. Akmal's sisters are already sitting around with different plates of chicken and fish in front of them. They all give me a smile and giggle as they wave. Despite having been here with Akmal more than once, I still feel awkward when his mother shoves me to sit by the girls.

"Makan. Makan. You guys look like you're starving. There's plenty to eat la. We will make sure you leave here full and give you some to take home." I'm practically rolling out of here when we're done with our visits with how much food they shove at us.

Malaysians eat with their hands, so I sit myself down and cross my legs to join in on their family meal. I've seen them cup their hands when they gather rice, so I try to mimic them when I eat. Akmal's mother has placed me by her oldest daughter again and I inwardly groan. She's a lovely and very friendly woman and all but...

"Mat, doesn't Hasanah look lovely today. You know she is of marriageable age and we already love you like a son. You guys would make beautiful grandbabies for us." Akmal's mother is sitting right by me as she tells me this, looking between her oldest daughter and myself like she's already planning the wedding ceremony. I can hear Akmal choking on his food, and his mother sends him a stern look.

Like every visit, I send a prayer under my breath that I survive this lunch without getting engaged to one of Akmal's sisters.

"Laugh it up, Mat. Why do you think I'd rather come over to your place so often? It's like walking to the guillotine every time I go home with their constant questioning and pestering about if I'm seeing anybody. I'm almost afraid to bring any girl I'm interested in around because they'll be planning the wedding before our arrival behind our backs."

"Hey man, at least you're surrounded by a family that loves and cares about you. Even if it seems like they care a little bit too much."

"Yeah, you're right. I shouldn't complain. But man, they can be a pain."

We both laugh and continue watching superheroes kick ass and save the world. Akmal knows about my past and never brings it up. That's why he's a good friend and an easy-going person I don't mind hanging out with.

Chapter Four

MAT

She cuffed me to the bedpost like a damn sacrifice. I'm glad I heal quickly because Miss Miller's eyes lit up when she saw my new tattoo. The little black switch she brought out of her closet makes me groan in dread on the inside because it means she's feeling feisty today from her excitement. Damn this job and damn this woman for always figuring out ways to sabotage her stuff to call in for service, always asking for me. It doesn't help that I actually perform my job to fix the issue, therefore no one at headquarters ever sees her cases as anything but what they are: cases to be solved and closed.

I should change that somehow. *Thwak!* The sting of her whipping me takes me out of my thoughts for just a second. I should really figure out a way to either offload her cases to someone or figure out a way to blacklist her from our company. I wonder if Akmal can help me brainstorm the latter. *Thwak!* Shit, I think she whipped my obliques. That shit stings a little worse than the last one, making a hiss escape between my teeth. Her smile is feral now and her eyes are dilating. She loves getting a reaction out of me since I work hard to not give her one.

Miss Miller isn't bad on the eyes. She's a full-figured, confident redhead. What hot-blooded male would say no to her?

Me. *I'm* that hot-blooded male that would say no. The only problem is that I was trapped in her web of lies and manipulation before I even realized no would be an option. I was naive and she took advantage of it. Took advantage of the fact that I don't like hurting women. Now I'm in so deep, some days that light at the end of the tunnel seems so hopeless.

I don't know what's going on in that mind of hers as she uncuffs my hands and forces them on her hips as she positions her pussy above my face. Do guys actually get pleasure out of being treated this way? Like a damn dog? She slaps my face when she notices me zoning out and I start to lap at her lower lips the way she's taught me. She starts to moan, grabbing my hair by the fistful as she rubs herself all over my face unabashedly.

"Fuck yes, just like that. Eat my pussy, lick it clean." I swear this woman is going to scar me for all women for the rest of my days.

Flicking my tongue on her clit, hoping to make her cum quickly so all this crap can be over with, her grip on my hair starts to get tighter, signifying her climax approaching. *Fuck, hurry up woman.*

Her body starts to shake a little as her pussy clenches over my tongue when I spear her one last time to push her over the edge. She squirts on my face like I'm a fucking toilet seat and I can't do a damn thing about it. She doesn't squirt often, but when she does she tends to be a little nicer to me for the rest of the time I'm here.

"Fuck...yes... you like that don't you. You like me dirtying you up with my juices. You're such a good boy." She loves petting me like I'm her puppy. I need her to get off my face.

My thoughts must be transmitting clearly from the last time I fixed her modem because she does just that, gets off my face and falls to her side on the bed in an unattractive heap.

I quickly get up and go hop in her shower before getting back into my work clothes. I need to get out of this stifling house. After what feels like a five-minute shower, I come out to see she's back in robe again, hair all mussed up from all the messing around we did... rather, all the messing around she forced me into. My cock is only semi hard and I'm glad for it because I don't want her anywhere near it today.

I don't even have the energy to say anything to her as I fix her 'IT issue' and run out of the house as fast as I can without looking like a crazy person to her neighbors.

Only when I shut the driver's side door do I breathe a deep sigh of relief before quickly starting the ignition and backing out of the driveway.

The neighbors I drive by all give me a disgusted look, since the screeching of the company car tires are probably leaving tread marks on their pristine roads. Well, screw them. I never liked their neighborhood, anyway. Too many bad memories thanks to a particular client.

When I make it back to the main building, I park the car in the designated employee lot and lean my head back to rub my scalp. Miss Miller almost ripped my hair out this time as she came on my face. My follicles still feel tender as I continue to massage my head in slow circles.

A knock on the driver's side window makes me jump. Akmal is pointing his finger down to tell me to roll down the window. I do and Akmal is giving me a critical once over.

"You alright, man?" Shit, if only he knew. Akmal only knows that I hate going over there and that she doesn't treat me right, but not about the details.

"Fuck, I can't take Miss Miller's cases anymore. We need to do something. Tricia can't be there to save me every day."

Akmal stands back as I roll the windows back up before exiting the car and leaning against the driver's side door.

With one hand on his hip and the other under his chin, Akmal and I both stand next to each other in silence as we try to come up with a plan.

Akmal surprises me when, a few minutes later, he snaps his fingers.

"Fuck, I got it! You need to buddy up with Travis on the next Miller case."

"Why the hell would I want to buddy up with a rookie? How is that going to help me?"

"Listen to me, man. I've only buddied up with that guy a few times and his need for attention and recognition is annoying as hell. Who better to give it to him than Miss Miller, eh?"

My eyes widen at his idea. Shit. It just might work.

"Shit, Akmal. This is exactly why you're my bro. Fuck yeah." We slap our palms together and bump each other's shoulders. I have to hold on to him since he almost topples over, but we're both laughing as we walk into the glass double doors.

"Hey guys!"

"Tricia? Aren't you off today?" She's dressed in normal clothes, so I don't know what she's doing here. I wouldn't want to hang around this place during my off-duty hours.

"I, uh, needed to talk to Morty about something. Since I was kind of in the neighborhood anyway, you know..."

"..okay. Well, I guess we'll see you tomorrow at work."

Morty walks out of the restroom at that very moment, still fixing his pants by lifting it up over his gut. He looks surprised to see Tricia here, too.

"Tricia, you're on schedule for tomorrow."

Tricia lets out a weird laugh and starts to say something to Morty. But I don't hear it since Akmal and I are both already walking away to the break room. We don't usually eat here, but we do sit down for brainstorming on where we should take our lunch if we have to.

"Hey guys! Wait up!" Akmal is still holding open the door as we both turn to see Tricia jogging towards us.

"You guys want to go get lunch or something?" She's staring at me when she asks this and I look back at Akmal. He shrugs, indicating he doesn't care whether or not she comes.

"Yeah, that's cool. We usually hit up Sammi's nearby. Akmal, you up for sandwiches?"

"I'm up for anything I can fill my stomach with. I'm starvin' like Marvin."

I chuckle. Well, that's settled then.

"Who's up for driving?"

"That would be me. You drove last time." Tricia smiles at me as all three of us walk back to the employee parking lot towards my car.

Opening up the passenger door for her, Tricia sits in the front passenger seat as Akmal crawls into the back.

We pick the same table outside when we get there, grabbing an extra chair from the nearby table for our extra person. Seems we also get the same waitress as well.

"Hey boys, what'll you have? The usual?" Her smile falls off her face when she sees the other guest that's joined us today. Suddenly there's a tension in the air and I can't understand what it's stemming from. Both Akmal and I are looking at each other discreetly with scared looks on our faces. How do you diffuse something when you don't even know what's wrong to begin with?

Tricia sends a strained smile at the waitress as she gives her her order, and the waitress sends a strained smile back.

Sheesh. Women are so hard to understand. Maybe they know each other?

We all eat in relative silence after our food is brought out. The strangest thing happens when the waitress brings our bill. She places it in front of Tricia and that weird tension comes back. I grab the bill when the waitress turns around and toss down enough to cover our food and a tip so we can leave before she returns again. I don't understand women, but I don't think I can sit through another session of whatever it is that's going on.

Chapter Five

ATSUKO

"Atsuko, are you going to make it to the vintage car show next weekend? I heard there's going to be a lot showing up on the fairgrounds this year."

"Of course! I actually scheduled a photoshoot with a freelance photographer. He was offering a good deal. Figured I should update my portfolio." Hopefully, this guy won't be as creepy as the last one I hired for the air show.

"Yeah? I need to do that too. I'll accompany you, maybe I'll hire him too if he's good." Veronica, Vero, is currently reapplying her Cherry Bomb red lipstick on her lips, pressing them together and making a pop sound in front of a mirror sitting on the makeup counter.

With her round ass sticking out and wriggling, more than a handful of guys have taken steps backward to do a double take. Vero has the best ass around, so I don't blame them at all. When an older silver fox starts to loosen his collar from afar watching her apply another coat of lipstick, I slap her ass, making her jump up and turn to look at me with a sparkle in her eye. She slaps my ass back, and I can hear the gentleman groan under all our laughter.

Vero and I have been best friends for the past fifteen years. We met one day at a classic car convention while photographers were asking us to pose for pictures for one of their calendar shoots. We hit it off like we were born sisters and with our mutual dark hair and light skin shade, you probably would think so as well if it wasn't for the difference in our nationalities. Where I am of Japanese American descent, Vero is Hispanic.

"What was that for?" Her words sound like she's mad, but her inability to hold back her smile tells me otherwise.

"You know what that was for. Shaking your ass like that. You're going to cause an accident near my workspace! Ain't nobody got time for that!" We both laugh because it's true, and she knows it. The makeup counter needs to be kept pristine to attract the customers. I work for commission for my day job and having Vero here on her days off to hang out helps a lot because she's a bombshell and her makeup game is on point. She always looks like she just stepped off the pages of a pinup magazine. It's our go to look when we're off work, tackling the world like we're double trouble. We're almost the same size, allowing us to swap clothes back and forth.

It's about time to change shifts with the next girl and I was able to make a few good sales today, thanks to Vero. Women would come by asking what product she used and she would tell them the names of all the ones I sold, despite not even wearing them on her face. She always has my back like that.

Bending over to grab my bag on the ground, a large warm hand covers my ass cheek over my pencil skirt with a caress. His other hand starts to travel from my waist to my abs over my top before his familiar voice carries to my ear.

"Shit, babe, you can't bend over like that in front of the public. I might end up in jail again."

Alfonso and I are on and off. Standing at about five-feet-nine inches, Alfonso's got the bad boy look down to a T because that's exactly what he is. To be honest, he isn't my man besides seeking each other now and again for mutual benefits, but he sure likes to act like he is whenever he's around. Always metaphorically pissing all over the place to stake his claim just because we tumble in bed together a time or two when I'm horny enough.

Come to think of it, I didn't even know he knew my schedule.

"Why are you here Alfonso?"

"Why you gotta be like that, huh? Can't I just come see my girl?" Now that I'm turned around facing him, his hands continue to take liberties at my lower back. I don't love it and I don't hate it. But I really don't want him to think this is something more than what it just is.

"Your girl? I'm not your girl. You're going to need to take your hands off me since I didn't give you permission to touch me." My eyes scan his five o'clock shadow across his jaw.

"I love that mouth of yours. You want to go back to my place?" He doesn't have a place last I remember. Alfonso's tendency to be in and out of jail makes it hard for him to have anything of his own.

"You mean take her back to Joaquín's house? Don't you get embarrassed banging my girl at some other guy's house? She deserves better than that." Vero is glaring at Alfonso with the corner of her lip curled up, because she *really* doesn't like him. She also knows that a girl has needs and Alfonso is the easiest catch when I need some D. Despite her five-feet-five stature, Vero's nature is to never back down from much when she's got her hackles up.

"Why don't you just shut the..." He shuts his own mouth up when he sees the daggers I'm starting to glare at him. I'll admit it, Alfonso can be a little uncouth. Who am I kidding? He can be a damn heathen sometimes. It used to get me going when we first hooked up. Now it gets downright annoying, especially when he's shooting that stuff at my girl.

"Baby, don't look at me like that. You know me. Sometimes my mouth goes before my mind does. Come on baby, I've missed you." He tries to grab onto my waist but I side step him just far enough away from his reach.

"You need to go Alfonso. I'm off work and I want to go home."

"Yeah, you need to go. Don't worry, I'll take care of Atsuko real good if she's got an itch she needs to scratch." Vero begins to caress my tits right in front of him. This crazy girl, that's why I love her.

Alfonso looks pissed because he's a possessive motherfucker, but he's not my man, and he knows it. When I feel her fingers start to pinch my nipples through my shirt and bralette, I squeak and slap her hand. We both laugh and hear a groan from somewhere nearby. Alfonso goes off stomping and growling on his way towards who I assume is the guy that groaned.

Vero and I take that moment to slip out from the vicinity, making our escape. Our laugh bubbles out of us all the way out to the parking lot like we're a bunch of teenage schoolgirls despite me being thirty five and Vero being thirty three.

"You need to shake that fool off. Alfonso is trouble. That boy is like a bomb about to blow every time he's around you."

"I know, I know. I've tried! He's like a stray dog, though. You give him a little and he keeps sniffing back for more."

We start separating ways towards our respective cars but continue our conversation anyway, with louder voices.

"Then stop giving it to him! Buy a million dildos if you have to, but do not take him back. Shit, if the itch still can't get scratched, you got me!" The sound of a loud crash nearby makes us both turn our heads just in time to see a teenage boy crash to the ground from tripping on the metal trash can. That's what he gets for eavesdropping.

"Mouths and fingers can only do so much you know?"

"Maybe what you need is a permanent boo. But that will never happen with Alfonso sniffing around."

"Can you please stop making sense? It pisses me off."

My keys are already in my driver's door before I hear Vero yell, "No it doesn't. That's why you love me. That, and because you love my tongue game!"

A few guys leaving their cars start choking on their drink but we pay them no mind. Vero and I wave as I get into my Toyota Camry and start the ignition. Vero's right. Maybe I need a permanent man, one that doesn't just want me for what's between my legs. I hate the dating scene. Since hooking up with Alfonso a few years ago, I never dipped my foot back in. Turning out of the parking lot and onto the street, I tell myself that maybe there aren't any good guys left out there.

Chapter Six

MAT

Tricia is off today. I volunteered to take Travis on my next call, which happens to be to Miss Miller's house. The plan is set in motion. I need to shake this woman off me. My soul can't take it. I should feel bad about what I'm doing. I really should.

"Man, I hope she's hot. Wouldn't mind some eye candy while we do work, right my man?" Right.

"She's one of our regulars. She's not too well versed in...technology and usually calls in trouble pretty frequently. They're usually easy jobs. If you want, you can go do this one solo."

"Yeah, I'm down for that. I don't need all this training Morty has me going through. I've done IT before; I know what I'm doing." And so the trap is set. This kid's cocky enough to jump on any opportunity to show off his skills.

"Alright, I hear you. Yeah, let's do it then. You take this one on your own and I'll be in the car doing paperwork until you're done."

"Fuck, it's about time." I hope she eats you alive.

Driving through Miss Miller's neighborhood, Travis whistles.

"This place is fucking loaded with money. I bet it's loaded with desperate housewives too, you know what I mean?" His unnecessary lifting of his eyebrows irks me. How did this cocky bastard even get the job, or keep one, for that matter?

This time when I pull up to her driveway, I don't feel the same sense of dread I usually do. I'm actually laughing on the inside, but my face is calm on the outside.

"Are you sure about this? I can always go in with you just in case."

"Nah! I got this. Come on, man, I'm not that stupid. I know what I'm doing. You just sit back and I'll be out in a few, I guarantee it." Do you now?

"Alright, alright." I watch as he gets out of the passenger side with his tool bag. The confident swagger he has going as he walks up to her door. I know the moment she opens it because his mouth falls open and throat starts bobbing. A flash of a hand and she's pulled him in. The sound of the slammed front door making me breathe a sigh of relief.

Guess I'll be taking an impromptu break in the car. Taking my cell phone out of my pocket, I open up my browser. I've been to Miss Miller's house enough to know her network password, not that she cares one bit.

The last page comes up and there's a blue classic car right at the top, the kind of blue that was common in the fifties. Some are fire engine red, others have flame paint jobs. All of the cars are well taken care of with a shine that catches your eye no matter how old the model is.

Akmal sent me the link to the convention coming up where he will be doing a photoshoot with some of the pinup girls. I'll be off that day, but I don't know if I'm going to go. It doesn't seem like my scene. Plus, there will be way too many people there.

Glancing at the clock on the top left of my screen, it's only been ten minutes since the door slammed. I don't hear any screaming, so I keep on scrolling.

I wonder how my grandparents are doing on the reservation. I think about them every now and again, but I'm too much of a coward to contact them after I was banished off the land. Are they disappointed in me? Ashamed? Have they disowned me by now since I've turned my back on our people and left without another backward glance?

Shaking the depressing thoughts out of my head, I think about my time working for Just Techs. I wonder if Morty even knows what goes on with these calls. I wonder if I'm the only one with a Miss Miller problem or if this is a common occurrence for the other guys? Nah, judging by their bored expressions when they come back from the field, it's probably just my bad luck.

Quickly getting bored, I do actually start catching up on paperwork. Once I'm all caught up, I tap my phone screen to check the time. Travis has been in there for about thirty minutes. Maybe it's time I check up on him.

Getting out of the car, I walk up to Miss Miller's front door and press my ear against it before knocking. I can't hear a damn thing, so I knock and turn the door handle. Seems Miss Miller must have been in a hurry because the door was unlocked.

The moment I'm halfway to her bedroom is the moment I hear, "You're a dirty little boy aren't you. And you fucking love everything I do to you."

Hopefully I didn't scar the poor kid for life.

When I walk closer to the bedroom doorway, I actually take a step back from the sight before me. Miss Miller is butt naked in heels, one of which is currently being pressed down onto Travis's balls as he lays there on his back on the ground with a damn smile on his face.

Walking lightly back towards the front door, I hear, "Suck my toes. Mmmmm, just like that. You're so dirty, just the way I like them."

With that, I make sure to close the door as lightly as I can so her attention doesn't turn to me. I should feel like a bastard, but I don't. That smile on Travis's face tells me he's right where he wants to be.

Another fifteen minutes later, a freshly washed Travis comes back to the car, opening up the passenger door.

"Holy shitballs. Is this what you guys do every day?"

"I don't know about the other guys, but Miss Miller is a regular. If you want, you can take her cases when they open up. She seems to have taken a liking to you."

"Hell yeah, I'd love to. That woman might break my dick off one of these days, but what a way to go." He laughs like he couldn't care less, and then winces when he moves a certain way. Thank fuck, because I could not care less that he's saddled with her. Things are starting to look up for me already.

Chapter Seven

ATSUKO

Vero and I decided to try out one of those dating apps that have become popular. She didn't want me to feel alone on this new journey and being the best friend she is, she hopped on the bandwagon without a hitch.

"Some of these guys look like they're using photos from their high school days. Come on, look at this guy! Age thirty-eight, but he looks like he's twenty? I don't believe it." Her finger swipes left as she continues to browse through the different pictures. Vero is a free bird like I am, another reason why we get along. We don't necessarily go out looking for men, men are usually in abundance around us, especially at car shows. I love dick just as much as the next girl, but when I have an available one a phone call away, I haven't really been looking.

"Some of these guys look like they have yellow fever." We both laugh because some of these guys do look like complete creeps.

We're hanging out at our apartment, in my bedroom. Our bodies are laid out haphazardly with some of our limbs hanging off the sides of the full sized mattress.

"My finger is going to get a cramp from all this swipe left shit." Vero dramatically groans as she drops her hands down to her sides from their upward position since she's lying on her back, her luscious locks spread all over the white sheets. I bump my shoulder against her but kind of miss since I'm lying on my stomach, still holding my phone between my hands. This crap is getting warm too. How long have we been doing this?

"Come on, you can't give up that fast. What if the right guy is the next one, huh?" Vero blows out a raspberry and turns her phone back on, lifting it over her head again at my suggestion.

We both stare at her screen. The next guy looks like a total creep who still lives in his mother's basement. Vero slaps me on the ass, and we both laugh uncontrollably on my bed, making it bounce. Damn, this dating stuff is hard. Or maybe we've just both been out of the game too long.

"This is exactly why I always end up back with Alfonso. What the hell am I supposed to do when I have an itch? Dating takes too damn long and if you jump the guy's bones on the first date, he will automatically think you're a slut, you know?"

"Alfonso is bad news, and you know it. That boy is on you like a man on crack. Addicted with no hope of recovery. With his history that can get dangerous."

"I know. I know." I groan because dammit, *I know,* but I don't know how to shake him off. But damn if his dick doesn't scratch that itch. My toys can only do so much! This is the curse of a woman who knows her body well. At thirty five, I have no shame for the cravings that come to me. I love my sexuality, I love that I love sex. It's finding the right partner, one that isn't a danger to you and your sanity and might snap at any minute. But maybe that's Alfonso's allure. The bad boy.

But that bad boy is also a loser, hanging out in his buddies' homes with nothing of his own. Ugh!

"Why are you groaning over there like that? Don't you dare consider that fool! His dick is not that great! Come on Atsuko!"

"I know what you're saying, but I don't want to just be jumping from dick to dick either, you know? It doesn't make it any better."

Covering my face with my forearms, I lie on my back and contemplate my sex life. Do I get a bigger dildo? What? What can I do? Toys really are not the same versus the real thing. The relief is so temporary. Maybe I just need a main man. A straight up constant boo to call my own, to ravish whenever the need comes up. Just thinking about it makes me scissor my legs. A big 'ol dick, constantly at my beck and call, one that knows how to work my body the way I like it.

"You don't have to jump from dick to dick when you have me."

Soft hands run up my knees to my thighs, gently pushing them apart. My body relaxes into the touch as the fingers grip the waistband of my cotton shorts, dragging both it and my panties down my legs in the slowest of motions. The cool air of the room caresses my hips and junction between my legs, making an enticing contrast to the atmosphere in the room that's starting to charge up with sexual tension. I can feel the goosebumps rise up on the surface of my exposed skin.

My breathing is still calm but slowly becoming deeper and deeper. My arms are still over my face, the restriction of one of my senses making all my other senses heightened. I love guessing what's next, lost in the darkness.

Once I'm naked from my waist down, the hands come back with a soft caress from my ankles to my mid thighs. Not so gently, the hands force my legs open wide and I submit to their command. I feel the light brush of her hair on my inner thigh before the heat of her mouth and tongue swirling on my clit. A tease with the tip, a tease with the flat of her tongue. Vero tortures me by pushing my sensitive bud with too much pleasure and then too little.

The room starts to feel stifling, my hunger growing with every movement she makes over my pleasure zone.

My hips start a slow dance, pushing itself towards her mouth, silently begging for more while still trying to remain submissive. When she covers my opening with her soft lips, her tongue darts out aggressively, invading my wet pussy with the muscle, making me moan. In and out, in and out with a flick of her tongue upwards. I widen my legs for her to get closer and deeper, making her moan against me; the sound vibrating against my lower lips increases the sensation that's already heightened.

She starts making out with my pussy like it's my mouth and slowly moves her lips over my clit again. The feel of one finger, then two enter me as her mouth and lips continue their attention on my clit and make my hips start to thrust against her even more. I feel like I'm going to combust into flames but I hold back my sounds, letting her take the lead, letting her tell me how fast she wants this to go.

It starts to feel better and better, my body chasing something that's so close and so far away at the same time. When Vero starts to flick my clit and sucks it hard, inserting a third finger at the same time, my body explodes and I swear I see stars behind my closed eyelids. She moans and continues to suck on my clit hard, almost to the point of pain. I love it. Her fingers never letting up on their thrusting against my pulsating pussy, her lips making way for teeth to join the party makes my aftershocks climb even higher instead of die down. *Fuck.*

Removing her fingers, her tongue travels down to my pussy and her nose grazes my clit every now and again as she licks up all my juices, making me squirm. I can feel some of it trail down to my back hole, making me clench my ass and pussy around Vero's tongue.

I feel her shuffling, the bed moving with her as she removes her mouth from me. Taking my arms away from my face, I watch as Vero crawls up my body, slowly removing her own clothes in the process. All that's left is her panties as she grabs one of her breasts and feeds her nipple into my mouth. My arms go around her, pulling her in closer so I can get a bigger mouthful of her beautiful tits in my face. Doing the same thing she did to my clit, I suck hard, twirl her nipple with the end of my tongue and nip at it in different patterns. Vero loves having her C cup breasts played with. So do I, but I'm too horny for her right now to think of me. I'm desperate to make her feel good, for her to use me for her pleasure.

She grabs my hair and pulls it back hard, making her nipple pop out of my mouth right before she shoves my face to her other breast, commanding me to satisfy her craving for breast play. I happily comply. The more I suck her nipple, the more I knead her other breast with my hands, the more she loosens her grip on my hair. She moans and bites her bottom lip, revealing just how much she's enjoying what I'm doing to her. I am too and I can feel myself get even wetter than I already am.

Her breathing is picking up and I love that I'm doing that to her. It makes me feel powerful.

"I need you to eat my pussy. Now." Her nipple pops out of my mouth as she quickly lifts her torso up and my inner nympho is purring in satisfaction, watching her nipples both glisten and look angry red from my kisses.

The room feels hotter and hotter, the air thick with sex, especially with both our bodies sliding against each other. She starts to climb again until she's sitting right over my face, her cotton panties sticking to her pussy from how aroused she's become.

Grabbing her ass with one hand and pulling the bottom of the panties aside with the other, I start to dip my tongue into her wetness. She tastes so fucking good, it's making me hot and horny all over again.

She leans back and tweaks my nipple hard, making me moan into her pussy. She's like this. She gets feisty when she's not getting what she wants from me. It's her signal that I need to up my game.

Grabbing her ass with both of my hands, I make her shove her pussy even lower on my face. My tongue continues to thrust into her, my lips and teeth nipping at her lower lips and clit every so often. One of my hands caresses her ass and squeezes it hard before it travels low enough to stick a finger inside her back entrance. Some of her juices have already traveled down, making it easy for me to rub it there. She tightens and then relaxes her hole enough for me to thrust my finger inside as she groans. She's getting wetter by the minute and the moment I tease her ass and add another finger, she cries out in pleasure and starts grinding hard on my face and tongue. I love how shameless Vero is with her body. She knows she's hot. She knows she's edible, and it turns me on. Her confidence only boosts mine, that's why we're best friends and roommates.

She continues to ride my face and tongue despite my fingers having been removed from her ass. When her body starts to go limp, she rolls to the side of me, onto her back, trying to catch her breath.

Getting up to clean my hands in the adjoining bathroom, I come back with a toy and lie right back next to Vero. She smiles and there's a wicked glint in her eye.

"You are such a slut. You can never get enough. I either feel bad or good for the man that catches you, Atsuko." We both laugh like psychos. Vero is the only person I allow to call me that. She knows I'm not a slut, I just love sex.

With the dildo in my right hand, I start to tease my lips and clit with the head a few times to lube it up before pushing it in me. I moan, my lips and insides still overly sensitized by what Vero put me through. The stretch makes me even hornier, making it glide in and out, in and out.

Vero rolls over and pulls my tank top down, exposing my left breast to her waiting mouth. She pinches my clit while she sucks, like she's waiting for milk to flow if I had any. Just the thought of that taboo makes my pussy clench around the girth of the toy. This is the difference. Vero scratches the itch only a little with her fingers in my pussy, but my pussy always knows the difference between what it really wants: a big dick inside to fill me to the brim.

My hand thrusts the dildo in tune with her sucks, and soon enough I let out a strangled moan when my climax hits me for the second time tonight, even harder than the first. When the beat of my heart starts a steady decline, I let out a satisfied sigh. My body feels lax. It feels somewhat satiated for the time being.

I watch with hooded eyes as Vero takes the dildo out of my pussy and starts to lick it up seductively in front of me.

"Ugh, stop! You know what it does to me."

Her tongue swirls around the crown of the toy and she laughs, falling back down on the bed beside me.

"Do you think I'll find someone who can keep up with me?"

"I don't know, Atsuko. But you'll never know until you try."

She's fucking right. She's always fucking right.

Chapter Eight

MAT

I don't know what happened, but Miss Miller started asking for me again. Travis has been to her house for the past few days and it seems he's already worn out his welcome. How can this be? I thought they were doing good together? How did this fool mess up a thing like that?

"Hey! Are you going to Miss Miller's house? Let me tag along."

"Who are you supposed to be buddied up with right now?"

"Bradley, but he wouldn't mind." I don't trust this guy and anything that comes out of his mouth.

"Yo Bradley!"

"What's up?"

"You don't mind Travis buddying up with me on this case?"

"Shit. Take him." Seems like Travis is wearing out his welcome in more places than one.

"I got you. I'm going to take him on my next one."

Bradley nods without even turning around. He doesn't care where Travis ends up. They must have butted heads about something for Bradley to act that way. He usually gets along with everyone.

"Sweet!" Travis is rubbing his hands together like a kid that just won a candy prize.

When we reach Miss Miller's house, I decide to try my luck and get out with Travis. I need to understand where it went wrong, why she's decided to request me again when she has a willing victim right here.

Travis looks like he's going to jump out of his skin with how his steps are bouncing the closer we get to her door.

The air shifts as she opens the door to greet us in her signature black robe and hair bun. The smile she shoots at me is lecherous, dying down when she turns to see that I'm not alone. Damn, this guy really messed up somehow.

"Well, come in, boys." Am I really doing this? Maybe she won't do anything with both of us here.

"Don't mind if I do." Travis is already walking past the doorway as Miss Miller continues to stand there, looking me up and down. It makes me feel like spiders are crawling all over my skin, but I try to give her a smile anyway, being on the job and all.

When I enter her living room, the sound of the door shutting and lock engaging makes me close my eyes and take a gulp. When I open them back up, Travis is already halfway stripped out of his clothes. My god, does he have no shame in how desperate he looks right now?

My eyes widen when he gets onto his hands and knees, butt naked and starts crawling to her. A smile creeps up on her face and her attention is off me, thank heavens. She opens up her robe just as Travis reaches her and shoves his face between her legs.

Quickly, I check out the IT problem, fix it and start plastering myself against the walls away from them. Maybe the shadows will help make me invisible as Miss Miller throws her head back and moans the more Travis licks her.

My hands are reaching out for the front door lock when Miss Miller gasps, making my eyes shoot to her position. My heart slams into my chest, thinking I got caught when in reality Travis's hands are kneading her ass, making her widen her stance against his face.

Quickly and quietly unlocking the door, I escape and close it back before anyone realizes I'm gone. The sounds of her moans silenced by the seal of the door.

Wiping the sweat off my forehead, I rush back into the work vehicle and shut the door for some security, making sure to lock it. Leaning my forehead against the steering wheel for a moment, I let my heart rate come back to normal before taking out my phone and relaxing for my impromptu break.

It seems I haven't changed the page on my phone's internet browser because when I open up the app, the classic cars are there again. I decide to text Akmal and see how he's coming along with preparing for that photoshoot since it's scheduled for this coming weekend.

> **Me**: Hey! Are you ready for the photo session this weekend?

> **Akmal:** Yeah! I'm still kind of nervous. You down to go with me in case I need some assistance?

> **Me:** Man, I don't do well with crowds. I'm not the most sociable person.

> **Akmal**: I'm not either! You can just be my backup IT guy in case my laptop jacks up while I'm shooting photos. Heck, or just stand in a corner so I don't feel alone.

> **Me:** I don't know.

> **Akmal:** There will be HOT girls there. Like smoking. You shouldn't miss an opportunity like this.

I don't know how Akmal does it. His culture doesn't even let him have any sexual touches or relations before marriage, yet he's going to go do a photoshoot with a bunch of attractive women walking around wearing who knows what. I wouldn't be surprised if he ends up in the hospital for a bad case of blue balls after this gig.

> **Me:** That's true. But I suck at talking to girls too.

Akmal: Who said you need to talk? Just stand there, man. One of them is bound to come up to us to ask for a photo at least.

Me: LOL

Glancing at the time on my phone, Travis has been gone for thirty minutes. The sound of the door makes me turn my head to look out the driver's side window. Speak of the devil. He's kind of limping but looks relatively unharmed.

He slowly sits himself on the passenger side and winces when he reaches for the door to close it. Well, he knew what he was getting into.

"All good?"

"Yup." Alright then. Starting up the car and backing up, the drive back is a quiet one.

Chapter Nine

ATSUKO

Vero's on duty today behind the bar at the local Cuban restaurant, Havana Palace. It's not too posh, so I come to hang out with her when I'm off and the manager doesn't mind during the slow times. Both of us have our day jobs, but our hope is we get picked up for a contract through modeling that we wouldn't need our day jobs anymore.

Vero and I have done a few magazine shoots but getting picked up for something like a pinup clothing line would be a nice and steady income.

"What are you going to wear to the convention, Vero? Can I borrow your red pumps?"

"Of course, chica, take whatever you need. I think I'm going to wear the black wriggle dress so I can showcase my ass-sets, you know?" We both chuckle at that because Vero's got some good assets indeed, the perfect hourglass shape in a dress like that.

Maybe we should go as twinsies. "Alright, I'm going to grab the wriggle skirt jumper and a white top. Your red pumps will help the outfit pop."

"Don't forget to wear a red bra so we can see a peek. I bet it would look hot on the photoshoot." That's a damn good idea.

Taking a sip out of my water on the counter, we watch as the customers come in and out. It's still a little early to be drinking, so Vero has lots of time on her hands. Leaning over the counter to whisper to me, I can see her cleavage almost spilling out her button top.

"Maybe you'll find some good D there. Lots to choose from. Then you can finally kick Alfonso to the curb."

"We shall have to see." I'm not too fond of the idea of jumping on some random cock. What if it's not even good? This is why I always find myself going back to Alfonso time and time again. He knows my body. What is wrong with me?

"Hello ladies. How are you today?" I take another long sip of water from my straw before turning to the right to see who's talking.

It's a handsome guy, looks like he's in his mid-twenties. A five o'clock shadow graces his face, contrasting nicely to his smooth, wavy brown locks. He's looking from me to Vero and back to me, trying to decide who to hit on. Since Vero's tits are currently on display, he decides to face her fully. I couldn't care less, but this is exactly why I'm kind of scared to venture away from what I know. This guy looks like a five pump chump.

What if a guy only pretends to want me because of what's on the outside? I know that's the point of a hook-up, but I can't help but feel weird about it. At least with Alfonso, we've known each other for so long, I know it's not just for what's between my legs. Hence why he always tries to 'get back together' and make me 'his girl'. It was good while it lasted between us but he continues to have no prospects. I love myself too much to settle for that.

I must have been musing in my own mind for a while because Vero and the gentleman have already disappeared some-where. Hopefully, she keeps it down so the manager doesn't come out to check on what's going on.

What kind of man *do* I want? I've been riding the solo train for so long, I never really took the time to think about it. Being in my mid-thirties, I guess I should. Where does one even start? How do you know you're not setting your stan-dards too high or too low? Alfonso's got one thing going for him besides his cock, he's a one track minded, devoted guy. He does teeter on dangerous territory when he's under the influence, which is usually when I avoid him.

I wish things could be simple, like a notification that pops up in our mind when our soul mate walks by. Is that too much to ask?

I'm just about done with my water when the gentleman from before walks past me quickly and winks at Vero who is still fixing her hair and top. Trying to suppress my smirk, I look down into my cup to gather myself. My my. That was a quickie.

"How was it?"

"Eh, good enough for a quickie. I mean, he's a little young. He rams really hard and deep, I'll give him that." I swear this girl and her descriptions. She doesn't even keep it to a whisper in case anyone else walks by. I'm just glad she's smart enough to always use protection.

"Well, I'm going to head back home to message the photographer again one last time to make sure everything is a go. I'll see you there later?"

"Yup! Stay safe on the way home." We kiss each other on the cheek before I head out the door.

———

MAT

Fuck, Travis has got to be doing something wrong because Miss Miller is requesting me *again*. Why can't I shake this woman off? Isn't a willing dick good enough?

We pull up into her driveway and I'm actually getting a little ticked off this time around. Both Travis and I get out of the work vehicle and walk towards her front door. I re-knot the bun on my new undercut. It was a celebration haircut when I thought I got rid of Miss Miller forever. Seems my celebration was done a little too early.

She doesn't open the door when we get there this time, so I actually have to knock. My fists may be a bit heavy-handed with how I'm feeling. She opens up on the second knock, my fist still hanging in the air. Her smile is a different one. I can't decipher it just yet, but I'm on edge anyway because this is

Miss Miller we're talking about. She's got a lot of tricks up her sleeve.

"Miss Miller, very lovely to see you again." Travis is trying to smooth talk on his way in, but she hasn't shifted her eyes to him yet. They're tracking me like I'm prey, and my fight or flight is starting to make me antsy under my skin.

The days I was able to shove Travis in her direction was a taste of freedom I got used to. Now I don't want to give it up.

"Miss Miller." I nod my head and say no more, hoping she'll just tell me what the problem is, the reason for the call this time.

"I seem to have lost my cable. Help a lady out and maybe crawl back there to see if it slipped somewhere out of my reach?" Tricky, tricky fox. She wants me on my hands and knees, in a vulnerable position below her.

"Travis, can you check that out?" I never take my eyes off hers either as I give Travis the command. You can't take your eyes off a predator that's issuing a challenge. Seems we're at a small stalemate because Miss Miller bites her bottom lip, trying to think of another way to make me do what she wants.

Is that a crack in her control? It's making me feel things, but by the look of it, it's making her feel things too...things I don't want her to feel about me.

Travis takes that moment to crawl back out, still on his knees, towards Miss Miller as he hands her the wire she tried to hide. He's rubbing on her thighs, but she hasn't taken her eyes off me yet. She needs to just take what's offered to her on a platter and leave me the hell alone because I'm getting kind of tired of it.

Crossing my arms over my chest, I can feel my face frown at her determined look. What is it about me that makes her chase me so? I'm nothing. Just another male. She can have anyone else.

Travis is noticing the tension between us and decides to stand up in front of her, grabbing her face with both of his hands and forcing a kiss on her. Good. It's the moment I make my move and exit the front door.

Chapter Ten

ATSUKO

It's the morning of the car convention. Vero and I have been primping in front of the full-length mirror for a hot minute. I decided on the classic Hollywood waves in my hair while Vero is sporting some victory rolls.

We match with our dark hair and our similar choice of dark attire, but my red pumps help make me stand out. We both have our fire engine red lips on. The corset inside our outfits is cinched to create the perfect smooth hourglass and tight waist.

"Let's take the Camry, it's more comfortable than your clunker."

"Shut up ho, that clunker gets me to and from work." We laugh because it's on its last leg.

"Yeah, for now. And you don't have any triple A insurance for a breakdown."

"Chica, you're supposed to be my triple A." *Pffttt.* What if I can't get off work? This is why we take on photoshoots for extra side cash. Building up a good portfolio helps with getting gigs. Vero's family is very close, but she doesn't like asking them for anything since moving out. Trying to keep the independent woman thing going. Her parents are proud of her anytime they talk to her on the phone, always inviting us over for some homemade meals.

After placing her cat eye sunglasses on, she slaps my ass, making me squeak. She can't keep her hands off me. We walk out together and the cat calls start. There are some bachelors that live in our apartment complex but their fratboy lifestyle is such a turn off.

Putting my own retro sunglasses on, we ignore the neighbors and gracefully get into the camry and drive out of the neighborhood.

Vero bends over towards the console and puts on some Imelda May. Her voice and beat fill the car and it gets us in a relaxed mood. The trip to the convention is about a thirty-minute drive. The weather feels wonderful, so we put our windows down while we cruise and take our time watching the scenery go by. The scarfs on our heads help to keep our hair from going nuts before we can even arrive at our destination. The breeze caresses my cheeks like a lover's palm.

The closer we get, the more the parking lot looks full, the smell of vintage car exhaust filling the air. It's a nostalgic scent. These fairgrounds usually host the county fair during certain times. It's the perfect size for a car convention, allowing all the classic cars to have space between each other.

Finding a good spot, we pull in and throw the car in park. Stepping out with grace, one extended foot after another. These shoes make our legs look a mile long and we know it. The way the fabric clings to our curves, molding against us like a second skin.

Seems the men and their show cars are the ones arriving first. Some are accompanied by their women, but most are not. Most have their eyes trained on our legs as we swing our hips like we're walking down the catwalk.

The first building we enter holds some of the old model A and T Fords. Their paint is glossy enough to use as a mirror. Some of the older men enjoy these, smiling and winking at us as we walk by. I smile and Vero is blowing kisses randomly.

Exiting the building through the back, we come upon the muscle cars. These get our girly bits going. The age range of the owners is more our speed. Some of these silver foxes with their slick back hair and long beards can make a woman internally combust. One of them is blowing a kiss my way and I blush, fanning my face to cool it down. Some of the guys are younger and full of tattoos, their arms bulging against their button-down shirts as they cross them when we walk by.

Vero laughs at some of the men trying to get our attention, just soaking it up, as we continue walking around the cars until we see some of the lingering men on the side with their DSLR cameras and different lenses. The freelance photographer I'm supposed to meet up with named Mohd Akmal around this area.

We slow our steps and stare for a minute. There are about five guys here and only one guy kind of looks like a Mohd Akmal, but I don't want to make assumptions.

The five-inch heels put me at about just shy of six feet tall. A very friendly-looking man with light facial hair who is standing at least five inches shorter than me walks forward from the group. He bows in greeting, and I find myself smiling. This is different in a nice way. His eyes are never lecherous or going over our assets as he introduces himself as my photographer. I have a good feeling about him already.

"Hello ladies. Where would you like to start, Miss Kobayashi? Did you have a particular location in mind already?" Look at this guy, so polite. His Nikon is hanging off his neck and a messenger bag is slung behind him. Very cute in a nerdy type way. You just want to put him in your pocket. Vero seems to agree because she's trying to get his attention by canting her hips to the side a bit, but he seems to be immune to her charms and her bountiful breasts.

"I think we walked by a fifties Packard Clipper on the way here. How about we start there?" He looks clueless despite still having the friendliest smile on his face. Trying to stifle my laugh, Vero and I lead the way.

"He's so adorable. He wouldn't even look at me when I was bending over, did you see that? I can't believe they still make them like this." Uh oh, looks like Vero's got her eyes on this one.

I slap her arm to make her tone down her voice. "Girl, you are so bad. Leave that poor man alone. If you distract him, he might mess up my photoshoot." We both giggle because Vero is unstoppable when she's got her mind set on something.

After a brief conversation with the car owner who looks like he could double for Vero's dad, the photoshoot starts. Simple poses like leaning my hip back and leg up to bending over the hood. Vero even photobombed some of them, the bitch. We laughed it off since Mohd Akmal was being so kind about it all. Vero is preening like a peacock every time he looks her way, only to deflate when his gaze doesn't linger.

He must be a strong-willed person to not notice someone as beautiful as Vero. That or maybe he bats for the other team. That would make more sense.

A few more shots in front of muscle cars, a few with me laying on my back on top of the back trunk with my legs pointed towards the sky. I'm feeling pumped up because this guy seems to really have a good eye for this. He even let Vero sneak in a few professional ones with me with a smile. *Maybe he doesn't bat for the other team after all.*

"Alright ladies, I actually asked one of the car owners if we could borrow his Plymouth Barracuda. I think that's what he said."

Oh, this sounds *fabulous*. That's a hot car.

"He parked it in one of the smaller buildings on the lot. Let's head over there and out of the sun, shall we? My buddy is supposed to meet up with me to help me with the computer in case anything goes awry. My personal IT guy."

Our heels click on the ground at a steady pace as we follow the photographer to the designated location. It's much cooler inside the building from the shade it provides. Good, because I think I'm starting to glow a bit from the sweat.

Akmal is putting his messenger bag on a table that is sitting to the side while Vero and I cool down by the car, fanning our faces with our hands. A large and very tall figure walks in and goes directly behind the table to help the photographer set up his computer. His complexion is similar to Akmal's, perhaps a few shades darker but his high cheekbones, thick eyebrows over his very dark eyes, and strong nose are what sets him apart from his nationality. There's very light stubble on his face, shadowing the angles of his lower features. His undercut and hair bun only further highlights his cheekbones, making him look quite attractive.

He hasn't looked our way yet. These guys are a different breed than what we're used to. It's refreshing and strange all at once.

My eyes continue to track his movements, watching the way his shirt would stretch across his firm chest when he reaches for something on the floor from another bag. How can a simple t-shirt and jeans look so filled out on a person? His shirt is still loose enough to make a woman curious as to what other artwork lies beneath.

Akmal is still figuring something out with the buttons on his Nikon in my periphery, but my eyes have never left the vicinity of the newcomer. I can hear Vero trying to talk to the photographer, distracting him from what he needs to do. The IT guy brings his eyes up once and catches mine. It feels like time slows as we both stare at each other for however brief a period it is before he casts his eyes back down.

A shy one. I'm intrigued.

"Alright ladies, let's just do a few shots and we'll be good for today."

I position my ass leaning against the Barracuda, making sure to stick out my chest while my hands drift down to my cleavage right above the bow on my top. My head is tilted back and I'm thinking of orgasms as my lips lightly part.

Click click click click.

The shutter speed on the lens clicks in rapid succession with every slight move I make to change position. Getting into the driver's side of the Barracuda, I bring my legs up over the steering wheel, making sure to cross them and point my toes while staring out the front window right at the IT guy. His eyes don't give away any hint of what's going on in his mind as he stares right back at me from behind the laptop's monitor. No smile, no hint of anything on his face.

I can feel my pussy clenching at the thought of this little game we're playing. The subtlety of it all. He's proving to be a challenge and I like it. My lips lift into a coy smile, showing him that I see exactly what he's doing. Staring at me when he thinks no one is looking.

Click click click click.

"Alright! These look great! I'm going to have Mat download the digital images, making the raw preview available for you soon. I will message you once the photos are touched up and ready for your portfolio. Thank you so very much again for your time."

I can hear Vero gushing over some of the pictures he's showing her on the viewscreen behind the camera while I slowly bring my legs back down to the floorboards of the car. Stepping one heel out and then the next, bringing my body out of the driver's side. My ass shuts the door with a loud metallic thud, making Mat's eyes drift to mine for only a second.

I'm thinking about what it would feel like to run my hands through Mat's luscious black hair when I hear a voice I didn't want to hear today.

"Atsuko, what the fuck? I've been looking everywhere for you!" His words are running into each other a bit. This isn't good.

"What are you doing here Alfonso?" This is starting to get a little annoying and creepy how easily he can track me down. He doesn't even have a damn car. Did he take the bus all the way here...like that? Or did Joaquín drop him off?

"No one invited you to this shoot, Alfonso." The tension in the air is starting to amp up when my BFF starts to lift her lip at my ex. She really doesn't like him.

The closer Alfonso gets to me, the more he smells like he's had a few drinks prior to finding me. That's never a good sign. He already has no filter as it is when he's sober.

The corner of my eye catches Mat quietly stand up, staring at the scene from his table. The photographer has started to back up towards his laptop at the same time Vero is starting to place half of her body in front of me.

"Get the fuck out of my way, Vero. Ain't nobody here for you." Yeah, he's slurring a bit. His speech is a little bit slower.

"I'll get out of the way when I feel like it, fool. You need to back the fuck up yourself."

"Alfonso, you need to get it in your head that we're not together. We haven't been for years. You need to go, please, before you make a scene." Hopefully, by keeping a calm voice, he remains calm as well.

"Go? Make a scene? I'm not leaving you here with two men and this chick."

"Excuse me?" Vero's attitude is starting to seep into her voice.

There he goes, metaphorically pissing all over the place again to mark territory. I need to stop feeding him scraps because he's not letting go. This is my fault.

"Is there a problem here? I think I heard the lady say she wanted you to go." A deep voice I don't recognize gets closer.

Alfonso is snarling as he turns around to face Mat, who stands at least half a foot taller than him with a much broader build, despite trying to hide it behind his loose t-shirt.

"You need to stay out of our fucking business. I'm talking to my girl."

"I'm not your girl." Let's just clarify that again.

I don't know what Alfonso was going to do or say to that when suddenly Mat grabs him by the throat before he can turn to me and slams him onto the ground. My heart is beating rapidly, both of fear and excitement. Wow. Mat is one strong mofo.

Vero and I both take a step back, watching what happens next.

Mat's voice hasn't changed one bit from his calm demeanor.

"I'm not going to tell you again. You smell of whiskey and it gets on my nerves. I'm going to ask you to leave."

Mat literally picks Alfonso back up by the scruff of his shirt and tosses him towards the doorway to the building. Wow.

Our eyes clash one more time when he turns around before Mat turns back to the laptop to pack things up like nothing happened. How can he be so calm right now? In fact, Akmal doesn't look that worked up either.

"Well, thank you again, ladies. Miss Kobayashi, I will make sure to message you with the raw images and finished product as quickly as possible. Would you like us to walk you back to your vehicle?" Wow, still so professional.

That was very nice of him to offer, but my eyes haven't left Mat's back. He hasn't turned around, but I thought I saw his shoulder stiffening a little bit with the question. Interesting.

"Yes, I think we would like that very much, thank you." I think I would like to know more about this IT tech of his.

"Fuck yeah, I don't want to run into that fool again." She's right, I don't either. Not when he's like this.

Akmal tucks his laptop back into his messenger bag and walks to the right of Vero, while Mat silently walks to the left of me, making sure us girls are in the middle. My heel gets caught on something at the threshold of the entrance, and my hand automatically shoots out to Mat's bicep to prevent me from falling. *My god, his arms are firm.*

When I lift my head to look at him, I can see just how dark his eyes are. Secrets that are buried within the shadows of his face. His eyes look like they're tracking my jaw and then the slope of my neck, making my face heat up. Guys hit on me all the time, but it never feels like this... with just a look, Mat makes me feel a little speechless. I didn't realize that his arm is also around my waist while my hand is still on his bicep.

We both clear our throats as we detach and catch up with Vero and Akmal.

Chapter Eleven

MAT

I'm not sure what happened to be quite honest. One minute, I'm minding my own business trying to make sure the first session of photos are uploaded correctly to the right folders in Akmal's laptop, the next the smell of hard liquor burns my nose bringing back memories that makes my body tense up.

From the sound of their conversation, Alfonso must be her ex. *Her.* The beauty whose body looks like it was molded to replicate the gods. Her friend is practically molded the same but there's something about *her.*

I didn't pay her much attention in the beginning until our eyes kept connecting. Like a magnetism that draws me, calling me to look when I have no reason to, only to find her looking at me as well.

Getting rid of the ex was easy. I probably have at least fifty pounds on him. The smell wafting from his mouth makes my mind go into a slight haze, my fist wanting to meet his face. Since his exit was a smooth one, I was able to control the rage that was starting to simmer and boil into something. Especially since I saw how she reacted to him. She didn't want him there and it doesn't look like this is the first time he's been around her in this state.

Akmal was smart enough to offer to escort the ladies to their car. Females as delicate as these would be easy victims to anyone else who had too much to drink at this car show. When Miss Kobayashi, though I could have sworn I heard the guy call her something else, trips into me, my body starts to buzz from the contact.

Still kind of high from the adrenaline at throwing out her ex, my senses are heightened.

It felt like time stood still as we both locked eyes again. She looks as delicate as a flower with curves made for a man's touch. Any man would be lucky to have a woman look at them the way she seems to be looking at me now. I feel like a bastard for being privy to steal the glance she's giving me, like she's trying to wait out for something. What she's waiting for, I have no clue.

My hand can still feel the remnants of her warmth long after I remove it from the small of her waist. I'm not good with these kinds of interactions. I'm not sure what constitutes as pleasantries and what is too much. The good thing is, once Akmal and I escort them to their cars all that's required are simple goodbyes.

So why do I feel like I missed an opportunity for something? Once the ladies are in their car and drive away, Akmal and I slowly walk to the other side of the parking lot.

"These pictures are going to be amazing. Not only were the ladies gorgeous, they really knew how to work their bodies in all the right angles. It's not their first time in front of a camera, that's for sure."

"I didn't catch their names?"

"Oh, the Asian girl was Atsuko Kobayashi and I kept hearing her call her friend Vero."

Atsuko. Her name sounds almost as delicate as she does. How does hair even cascade in waves like that? Like a soft waterfall that falls past the beautiful slope of her shoulder.

"What do you have going for you tonight?"

"Nothing. It's my day off. That's why I decided to come to help out."

"You want to help me with the touch ups on the pictures? It will make the work go faster. I want to set a good precedent for my freelance work with efficiency. Maybe Vero can be my next client. She's got hips and ass for days, the perfect hourglass." So did Atsuko. They were almost like twin goddesses in their skin tight dresses and high heels making their legs look even longer.

What would it be like to have that softness against me? Miss Miller's face mentally takes over and my lips lift in disgust. I need to figure out a way to purge that woman from my system.

Following Akmal's car back to his place, we set up the laptop and camera to transfer the rest of the photoshoot. Sitting back in one of his office chairs, my eyes take in every detail of every single picture that uploads.

The close up headshots Akmal was able to take showcases the delicate freckles that kiss her face. The fullness of her red lips is a stark contrast to the color of her skin. She reminds me of a damn flower petal, delicate and smooth. Her long black lashes against her makeup and the hooded look she has on her face as she gazes out the car window straight into mine. It makes my dick twitch watching that look on her face without actually being a creep while doing it. I didn't want to make things awkward by staring when we were there, but now I can stare my fill.

"These photos are amazing, I don't think there will be much need for any touch ups."

Akmal scoots his chair towards the table and places his chin in one of his hands.

"I think you're right. These girls are a real beauty all on their own." A few photos of both the girls pop up and the way they bend over the car would bring any man to their knees to worship them.

"Damn. Vero is stunning isn't she?" Akmal's voice comes out in almost a whisper next to me. I knew he couldn't be immune to her, cultural dictations be damned. The poor fool isn't even allowed to touch himself.

My eyes are still glued to Atsuko on every single picture that uploads into the computer. "Yeah, she really is." Unlike

Akmal, I will most likely be touching myself tonight to these images.

"Alright, I'm going to put this in a network folder and grab the other laptop so we can both work on it at the same time. I'll take one batch and you take the other. Try to leave it as natural as possible and don't be afraid to ask me any questions if you have any. You've used photoshop before, right?"

"Yeah, I've messed with it here and there with gaming images. I'm sure I'll pick up on what you need me to do."

With that settled, we both start to work. Akmal must have a million shots of her. He told me to pick only a handful of good ones to work on. This is going to be hard when she looks beautiful in all of them.

We've been going at it for the past hour when Akmal excuses himself to the restroom. I don't know what comes over me but I shoot a couple off to my email so I can continue to stare at her in the comfort of my home. The moment I hit send, is the moment a message pops up from Akmal's photography website.

It's not my fault the window opens up all the way, showing me what's written.

A. Kobayashi : Thank you so much again for today, I really enjoyed the session. Cannot wait to see the final product.

MAB. Alqi : _

Do I dare? Akmal is still in the restroom and I'm burning with a strange desire to speak with her again. She doesn't even know it's me though. Does that still count as me speaking with her?

MAB. Alqi : It was great working with you as well.

The next message comes back quickly.

A. Kobayashi : It was also nice meeting your IT guy. Matt, was it?

My heart is kind of beating irregularly at this mention of me. Is she really asking about me? How would Akmal respond to that? I don't have to think about it when he comes waltzing back in, bending down to my screen to see what's going on.

"Oh good, she enjoyed working with me. Here, scoot over and I'll shoot off a message to her."

I quietly switch chairs and watch as he types.

MAB. Alqi : Yeah! He's my go to guy. You are correct, his name is Mat and he is currently assisting me with the photoshoot so that I can quickly return the finished product to you. Would you like a copy of some of the raw images now?

A. Kobayashi : Thank you so much, but that won't be necessary. I trust you will do amazing things with the finished product. My friend Vero wanted to know when your next available time slot would be?

Akmal has a big goofy smile on his face when he turns to me. Looks like he's got a crush on the Latin goddess.

"Dude! Her friend Vero wants to book a photoshoot with me. What luck! If I need you, would you be available? I'll make sure to do it on one of your days off."

"Is...her friend going to be there."

"Oh, shit. I don't know. I should ask."

> **MAB. Alqi** : That sounds great. I will have to get back to you once I look at my calendar. Will you be accompanying your friend the way she did with your shoot?

> **A. Kobayashi** : Most likely. We usually do come in a pair. How about we meet up to talk in person when you finish with the shoot from today?

"She wants to meet in person to schedule her friend's shoot. You got to come with me. I'm not good being with so many women at a table by myself."

"What are you talking about? Your family is huge. You're surrounded by women all the time. I know for a damn fact you guys have huge parties."

"Yeah, but that's different. They're family. These are hot girls. And from what I gather, hot single girls. Come on man, you got to come with me so I don't make a fool out of myself."

It wasn't like I was going to argue but I didn't want to look that desperate right away despite my heart rate kind of kicking up at possibly seeing Atsuko again.

"I don't know... I'm not good with social situations either. You know me."

"That's why we both need to be there! To buffer each other when it gets awkward. Come on man, do it for me yeah?"

Giving him a moment of silence so he thinks I'm deliberating it in my head, I take a deep breath and nod in agreement.

Akmal throws a fist up in the air. "Yes! This is almost like a double date, even though it's just to schedule a photoshoot."

Now that he mentions it, it is like a double date isn't it? I've never been on a date. My nerves are starting to get the best of me. Shit, what if I fuck this up?

Akmal's fingers are already flying over the keyboard.

> **MAB. Alqi** : That sounds great. We will most likely have the edits done by the end of this week. When would you like to meet up? And where?

It takes a good minute or two before she responds and I'm almost assuming she's bailing on us before it even starts. That would just be our luck.

> **A. Kobayashi** : Sorry about that. I had to work it out with Vero. How does this Saturday sound? There's a nice sandwich shop right across the street from the park. Do you know which one I'm talking about?

We both look at each other. I can feel the hairs on my arms lift up. She's talking about Sammi's? What are the odds? Is this a sign?

MAB. Alqi : Yea, we know exactly where that is. Sounds good. See you on Saturday.

Akmal is about to close the chat window to his website when one last message pops up.

A. Kobayashi : Tell Mat thank you for today.

I can feel a smile on my lips and it's the strangest thing. It reminds me that I probably don't smile as much as I should since my cheeks ache a little from how big I'm smiling now. I like that she's thinking of me. Granted she's probably not thinking of me the way I'm thinking of her. Shit, I'm going to have to jack off tonight.

We work for another couple of hours before calling it a night. Akmal walks me to my car and waves me off when I start pulling out of the parking lot.

Driving back to my apartment in the dark, I can still clearly see Atsuko's face and body in my mind's eye. I walk to the front door and living room in a daze, unsure of how I managed to shower and lay down on my bed when I don't remember anything but her face and the way she moved those hooded eyes in my direction behind the car's front windshield.

Shit, I don't think my dick is getting any rest tonight with her running around my head.

Chapter Twelve

MAT

The week went by quickly. Maybe because I've been anticipating Saturday. Tricia was able to divert Miss Miller's calls when she was on duty. When she wasn't, I told Morty that Travis was good to do solo trips in the field. He gave me a funny look but agreed. I never did find out what the issue was between those two. But he's still going over there so it must not be that big of an issue for her.

A whole week without Miss Miller and I'm already feeling like a new person. Travis hasn't complained one bit, so I don't feel bad about it.

"Are you ready for tomorrow?"

"Yeah, are you?"

"I'm excited and nervous. I hope she likes how the photos came out. I really hope Vero wants to work with me."

Akmal's been mentioning Vero's name more and more the closer we get to Saturday. I think the crush he has on her is starting to grow. I don't blame him. She's beautiful.

Just not as beautiful as Atsuko. Damn, just thinking about her name makes my dick twitch.

"Hey what are you boys talking about? What's happening tomorrow?"

"Nothing. Just stuff with my side gig."

"Oh" Tricia looks at me and all I can do is shrug. You can never have a decent conversation in this place without someone nearby listening. Both Akmal and I don't like people in our business. We like to keep our lives simple and drama free.

When Tricia gets tired of us keeping our mouths shut, she walks away. Good. Not before another person comes towards us.

"Fuck, thank you for passing your cases to me man. I love this job." Travis is out of his damn mind because no one likes working here, except for apparently him. I hope he gets his fill of that woman.

The rest of the day goes by smoothly without any other interruptions and Akmal and I say our goodbyes despite most likely talking to each other later tonight.

When I get home, my mind starts to overthink things and I start to think of all the possible ways tomorrow's meeting can go bad. I shouldn't think this way, but I can't help it. Good things don't normally come my way, not without an obstacle.

Hasn't my past taught me that? And anything involving Atsuko seems too good to be true.

She's probably not even interested in me that way and I'm just in over my head about stuff. Yeah, that's it. I log into the game chat and continue on with my nightly routine chatting with Akmal as usual without another thought about anything happening between a woman as beautiful as Atsuko and myself.

———

WE DECIDED TO CARPOOL ON SATURDAY, SINCE AKMAL IS all jittery about this date. Is it a date? It's basically a business meeting more like it.

We sit at our usual table outside of Sammi's. Our regular waitress is on duty today as well. The girls aren't here yet, so both Akmal and I only order water for the time being. Akmal tells me that he's been getting some inquiries since the car show. He was smart enough to hand out some business cards while he was waiting for the girls.

"You know, I might be able to do it. I might be able to do photography full time. I wonder where the girls are. What time is it?"

"You're going to have to chill, man." Akmal's knees are bouncing a little bit under the table, but it occasionally vibrates my glass.

"I just really want this freelance photography to do well, you know? It can be a solid full time job if it does. I can finally quit working under Morty." For some reason, Morty never got along with Akmal. Some days I think it's because he's jealous that Akmal knows more than he does and feels threatened by the potential of losing his position to him. With Akmal's friendly demeanor, he could probably run that company with better morale.

"I believe in you, man. You do good work, even a blind man can see it."

I feel a shift in my soul and it makes me look up. There at the far end of the street are two dark and beautiful angels coming our way. Is it possible that she's gotten even more beautiful since the last time I saw her?

Her dress is simple and flares out, swishing with her every step. The light colored little sweater she has over it only highlights her dark silky hair. Something is different but I can't put my finger on it.

I hit Akmal in the arm with the back of my hand and we both stand up before the girls can reach us. My hands are in the pockets of my jeans and the closer she gets, the more I feel like I don't deserve to be in her presence. She practically fucking glows.

"Hey! I'm so excited to see what you have for me!" Has her voice always been this soothing? My eyes never leave hers and when the girls finally reach our table, I realize what's different. She's much shorter than I remember. I glance down at her feet and she laughs, making my eyes shoot back to hers. There's a sparkle when she laughs and it draws me in. Am I smiling?

"I'm sure you've noticed. We're not in heels today." My arms itch to touch her but I can't. How can a guy like me touch an angel?

"Damn, I'm starving. Have you guys ordered yet?"

"Not yet. Here, let me get that for you."

Akmal and Vero's voices sound close but far at the same time. I can't seem to pull my eyes away from Atsuko's. The delicate shape of her face, the freckles I've memorized, the slope of her neck. Shit, am I staring? I'm acting like a creep even though I've stared at her pictures in my email all damn night.

Clearing my throat, I pull out a chair for her as she lowers herself to the seat. There's a small smile on her lips and I can't help but stare at how the edges of her lips tip up.

I can feel the heat on my face as I tear my gaze away and get back to my own seat next to Akmal.

The waitress comes out and takes our orders, quickly retreating back inside once Akmal starts to set up his laptop on the edge of the table.

"I've already sent you a copy of everything I'm about to show you to your email. If there are any problems opening them up, please let me know."

The girls are occupied for a short time, going through the gallery of pictures and I take a few moments to sneak in some more looks at Atsuko's side profile as I tip my glass of water up for a drink. Why am I so thirsty all of a sudden?

At this angle, I can see how the soft skin of her neck continues down to the hint of cleavage that peeks out from the top of her dress. I can feel my face heating up at the potential of being caught checking out her breasts. What the hell is wrong with me? But who could blame a guy? I'm only a man who has been placed in the presence of the most beautiful creature he's ever seen.

My eyes are staring at a particular freckle that sits near her collarbone when I hear a soft feminine throat clearing. It's so soft, I almost miss it. Atsuko is looking right at me, biting her bottom lip and my dick twitches in response. Swallowing down a groan by taking another sip of water, I turn my head to the side and hope she forgives my transgressions. I really suck at this social stuff.

Now that my eyes aren't on hers, my mind wanders to what Akmal mentioned earlier. He really could probably do freelance photography as a full time job. Where does that leave me? I'll be losing one of the only good things about that stupid IT job. What's holding me back? What other reason do I have to stay? I mean, I can do IT anywhere. Is it just the comfort zone of having been with this company for so long? That shouldn't be a good reason to stay because the place doesn't allow me to grow. Who the hell wants to work for Morty for the rest of their life?

"What are you thinking about so hard over there?" Her voice is like a siren's call, I don't have control over myself as I slowly turn her way. The soft smile on her face does something to my insides and it makes me feel nervous.

"Just work related stuff. Nothing important." Hopefully, my mumble was clear enough to understand. I'm saved from any more awkward conversation when our waitress places our food on the table.

Akmal and I eat in relative silence as Vero talks about ideas for her scheduled photo session. When the waitress comes by with the bill, I quickly grab it and throw down enough cash to cover all four of us and then some.

"Thank you, Mat." The sound of my name on her lips makes my dick strain against my jeans and I almost physically grimace when I tell her it's not a problem.

Akmal and I walk the girls back to their car. We learned that they are roommates, so they both came in the same vehicle. Akmal opens the passenger door for Vero and she gives him a bright smile making him take a subtle step back. I'm not sure what else I should be doing besides opening the door, so I stand there, waiting for her to get in.

She doesn't. Instead, she bites her bottom lip, distracting my thoughts again as she pulls me towards her by my front pockets. *Hot damn.* I almost stumble into her if it wasn't for my other arm shooting out to the top of her car because I didn't see it coming. She gets on her little tippy toes and my heart almost beats out of my chest. I bend down her way so she doesn't have to stretch so much. Her lips divert from my cheek and her breath caresses my ear with her message.

"Call me."

I'm stunned in place as she gets into the driver's side and closes the door with a *thump*. Akmal comes to stand by me and we both watch the girls drive away.

"Holy shit."

"Yeah."

"What was that about? I could almost feel the electricity in the air between you guys." I can say the same for him, though he was stepping away from her.

"I don't know. She told me to call her. I don't even have her number..." I go to stick my hands in my pockets again and feel something in my right front pocket. Grabbing it, I see that it's a slip of paper with her number on it.

"Shooo! You got her number now!"

That I do. I can feel my face smiling again as I stare at the beautiful script on the piece of paper.

Chapter Thirteen

MAT

My hands are clammy and I'm rubbing them against my jean-clad thighs. I don't know if I can do this. I shouldn't do this.

"Just do it, man!" Akmal's legs are bouncing next to me as we both stare at the ripped sheet of paper on my coffee table like it's an artifact in a museum of wonders.

"I don't know what to say."

"Hell, I don't either but you need to call her. She told you to."

"What do *you* usually say?"

"Hell if I know, I've never been on a date before." Look at us fools. The blind leading the blind. This isn't helping one bit. What if she didn't mean it? What if this was all an accident? What am I saying? She said to call her. I just don't know what to call her about. How do people do this kind of stuff all the time?

Bringing up my browser on my cell phone, I start typing.

"Are you calling her? Wait, are you putting it on speaker phone or something? What are you doing?"

"No, I'm googling how to ask a girl out on a date. I don't know how to do this shit."

"Oh, good idea. What does it say?"

We both lean in and start reading the different links about how to ask a girl out. After about fifteen minutes, I don't feel any less nervous but I think I got the gist of it. Alright, the websites say to keep it simple. Be prepared for rejection. Shit, that makes my stomach churn. But she gave me her number right? I really hope it wasn't a mistake.

We both lean back and I take a deep breath. Okay. Here we go.

My hands are shaking and I misdial the wrong number a couple of times. It's a good thing Akmal was next to me to let me know it was the wrong number.

When the right number starts ringing, I try to stabilize the phone next to my ear. My head feels hot and she hasn't even picked up yet. Does the number of rings before she picks up signify something?

When the sound of her hello comes on, my heart stops. Fuck, I can't do this.

On the second hello, I finally get the courage to take my head out of my ass and respond.

"Hey, it's Mat." Smooth, real smooth.

Her voice is almost a purr and it does something to me. "Hey Mat, I'm so glad you called."

I'm grimacing and Akmal is slapping my shoulder in a show of support.

"Yeah? Me too. Um. What are you doing next weekend?" This is it. This is it.

"Nothing, nothing at all."

My voice is shaking but I need to power through.

"You want to go out next Saturday?"

"Oh Mat, I thought you'd never ask. I'd love to go anywhere with you." Shit, my stomach drops because I didn't think it would get this far. I didn't plan on where to take her.

I cover the microphone with my other hand and frantically whisper to Akmal for some help. "Shit, where should I take her?"

Being the buddy he is, his fingers fly across the screen of his phone. When he's done looking for whatever it is he's looking for, he lifts it up so I can see.

"Mat, are you still there?"

"Yeah, sorry about that. Um, how about the uh..." Covering the microphone with my hand again, I glare at Akmal mouthing to him 'what the hell kind of place is that?'

"Shit, it sounded good. Just a burger joint, you know? Keep it simple, right?"

"How about I pick you up and surprise you." I'm too embarrassed to say the name Big Burger. Hopefully, she'll say yes.

She chuckles and it's the most feminine sound. "Sounds good. I like surprises. So, what time will you be picking me up?"

Damn, how many details go into dating? I'm sweating bullets. I turn to Akmal and mouth to him about a time. He's scrambling on his phone to google a good time to date. We're both sweating bullets.

"Mat, you are too cute. How about you swing by my place around seven. I'll text you my address. Vero wants you to tell Akmal she says hi."

Shit, she knew this whole time. I'm embarrassed but relieved she still wants to do this with me.

I try to chuckle like I didn't just get caught with my buddy stumbling over this dating thing. "Alright, sounds good. I'll be there to pick you up at seven."

"Goodbye Mat."

"Bye." My shaky finger manages to end the call. I toss my phone onto the table and put my face in my hands, running them through my hair. That was the most nerve wrecking thing I've ever experienced in my twenty nine years of life.

"Shit, you did it!" Akmal is howling and celebrating for me. I'm still waiting for my heart to come back down to earth. I can hear my phone ping with a message. It must be Atsuko sending me her address.

"She told me to tell you that Vero says hi."

Akmal chokes on his next howl and I have to slap him on the back a few times to settle him.

"Damn. I should have gotten her number. Then we could have done another double date, you know?"

That would have been much easier. But it isn't the case, and the date is already set.

"I need to keep her away from my family when they come by. They'll take one look at her and start making wedding plans and thinking of baby names." I chuckle at that because I can see it happening easily. Though judging by the way he acts around her, I don't think he'll be able to keep her away that long.

Once the nerves pass, I think about the job situation again.

"Akmal, what can a guy like me do with my skills? I don't want to be at the company forever. Once you leave, and you know you will, where does that leave me?"

"Sometimes, you just have to take a leap of faith. Comfort zones are known to be dangerous territory because they can blind you. What do you want to do?"

"I don't know, I guess I've never thought about it. I just work and go home."

"You know, I wouldn't mind having someone I trust to help me with this new photography endeavor."

"Yeah? But what do you need my skills for?"

"My website isn't the greatest. How about you come on as my Web Developer and Tech Manager."

I'm laughing because who the hell am I managing? There's only one guy in the company - Akmal.

"I'm serious Mat. After passing my business card around at the car show, I've picked up at least ten more shoots. We can do this. I can probably squeeze in even more jobs if I knew I had you at my back, so I can just concentrate on the camera work."

I am liking this idea more and more. There's a freedom in it, a freedom I never knew I needed.

"Shit, Akmal. We really doing this?"

"Yes, man! Why not? We're not getting any younger. No time like the present. We can even change the company name if you want. I'm not that big yet."

"Nah, you don't have to do all that. But yeah, I'm in. When were you planning on quitting with Morty?"

At the mention of his name, Akmal makes a disgusted noise.

"Shit, as soon as possible. I got some money in savings that will float me until I get both feet on the ground. How about you?"

"I've been doing nothing but working and going home. I have a good cushion in my savings as well."

"Let's do this then."

Fuck yes. I get up to grab the calendar off my kitchen wall and bring it back to the coffee table. We both stare at the dates and start deciding when we should put in our two-week notice.

Chapter Fourteen

MAT

Did I think I was nervous when I called her? Shit, it doesn't compare to what I feel right now as I pull up near her apartment. I'm really doing this. I'm going on a date with Atsuko.

Akmal tried to help me out with what to wear, but in the end we were so clueless that I just went with whatever was clean and within hand's reach.

I smooth down my button shirt when I get out of the car and try not to trip on my way to her front door. My knuckles hit the wood softly as I clear my throat in preparation for a smooth greeting. I read somewhere that showing up with flowers was a good thing, I'm just praying my fists don't clutch the stems too tightly and damage them.

I'm about to knock again when the door opens and her smell reaches my nose. It's something soft, subtle and slightly floral making you want to lean in to take a good whiff. I shouldn't though because that would be creepy, right?

When did my eyes close? I open them to find her absolutely glowing in front of me with her hair in a ponytail with a curl on top of her head reminiscent of the fifties. She's in heels again, making her closer to my height. The eyeliner she has on only emphasizes her beautiful brown eyes. She doesn't even look like she has much makeup on and it only showcases her natural beauty even more. Her dress clings to her curves in all the right places and is smoking hot red.

Her voice is purring again, the way it always does when she talks to me. Does she sound like this to everyone she talks to?

"Mat, you brought me flowers." I was starting to question myself about the decision until her beautiful lips pull up into a smile and she takes the bouquet from my hand to bring to her delicate nose.

"I've never had anyone bring me flowers before." Her smile is now blinding and I almost forget my voice for a second as I stare at how it transforms her face.

"Then we should remedy that."

"Yowza! Mat, you clean up well. Is Akmal around?" Why would Akmal be around if I'm just here for my date?

"Ignore Vero, she can't stop talking about him. You might as well tell him to call her."

"He doesn't have her number."

"Vero, you didn't even give him your number. Make sure you get on that." Her eyes never leave mine as she hands Vero her flowers, steps out and closes the door behind her, not waiting for her friend's response.

We start walking towards the car when I see some of her male neighbors peek out their door to look at her. Irrational anger flares up and I'm feeling kind of possessive as my hand covers the small of her back to make her walk in front of me blocking her perfect ass from their sights.

I caught her first. They shouldn't be looking at what's mine.

She chuckles at something as her hips continue to sway with her walk to the car. Opening up the passenger side door, I watch as she gracefully slides inside, one long leg after another. Holy shit, how did I get so lucky?

Trying not to slam the door, I run to the other side to get in as fast as I can.

The burger joint is already programmed into my phone's GPS in case I don't remember how to get there. Akmal and I did a few dry runs just in case, so I don't think I'll need to turn it on.

When we pull up to the parking lot, I'm having second thoughts again. She's dressed much too pretty for a place like this. It looks like a small diner.

"I love Big Burger! How did you know?" I refrain from wiping the sweat off my forehead because this could have gone so many different ways. I'm glad it wasn't a bust.

"Just a lucky guess."

"Vero and I come to this place all the time. I love the vintage atmosphere."

I have no idea what the atmosphere is like since I've never stepped foot in this place before. Opening the front glass door for her, I immediately see what she means. It's like a throwback diner with its black and white tile floors and retro decor. There's even a colorful jukebox in the corner.

Sliding into one of the empty booths, we place our orders to the nice waitress who comes up to our table. This is the moment Akmal and I have been training for. We've been practicing with each other on how to do small talk. I'm feeling confident. I think I can get through this date unscathed.

"Mat, just relax. I won't bite unless you want me to." Everything I've practiced and learned has gone up in smoke with that sentence. What the hell do you say to that?

She chuckles as I cast my gaze down at the table, trying to figure out how to steer the conversation back to more comfortable ground.

"So what are your interests?" There. That should get us back on track.

Her smile makes me blush and lose my train of thought for a second.

"I'm interested in you, Mat." Okay, Akmal and I have never anticipated this response.

"I'm interested in you as well." That's good, right?

"I'm glad." I'm saved by the waitress when she starts putting our plates onto the table.

We eat in relative silence. The food here is actually pretty damn good. I'm kind of glad Akmal chose it now.

"I need to use the ladies room." I nod my head as I wipe my mouth after taking my last bite out of the burger.

I notice the guy at the table behind us look her way and I glare at him until he notices me. He does and quickly averts his gaze back to his meal. Damn, is this going to be a regular occurrence? I know she's fucking beautiful, but keeping the other wolves from sniffing after her is starting to look like a job in itself. My gut tells me she's more than worth it. Maybe it wasn't a good idea to let her go to the restroom alone. An irrational fear and anger courses through me at the thought of some other guy cornering her at the restroom and taking advantage of her. Men can be damn animals when it comes to what they want to chase.

I toss a few bills down and quickly get up to go find her. There's a few guys lingering and it doesn't look like there's a line to the restroom. *I knew it.*

Being one of the tallest guys here, I shove my way inside the small hallway until the door to the ladies room opens up revealing my woman, safe and sound. She's still looking down at her little purse and I take the opportunity to glare at every fucker here, throwing in a snarl to the guys who glare right back at me. I'm about to punch the guy to the left of me for taking so long to bring his gaze up to mine when I feel Atsuko run into my chest.

My hands automatically go around her body to steady her but my eyes are still sending daggers into this fucker's head.

He's just lucky my hands are occupied right now. He finally sees me and scampers off. Damn straight.

"Oh, sorry. I didn't see you there, Mat. Have you been waiting here this whole time I was gone?"

My brain is telling me to remove my hands now that she's fine and safe, but my hands are refusing to listen. They're transmitting that this is exactly where they belong.

"Just making sure you were alright."

She laughs and I can feel that shit hit me in the chest. I should be the only guy to hear her laugh like that. It's a dangerous sound. There are too many men around here waiting to pounce.

"Why wouldn't I be?" Fucking hell, does she not have eyes?

"Because you're fucking beautiful and men are animals." The words slip out of my mouth before my brain is quick enough to filter it and she gasps. *Shit*.

"Are you an animal, Mat?" Are her eyes hooded? What the hell is happening here? My cheeks feel like they're flaming with embarrassment at my behavior.

I clear my throat and finally make my hands do as they are told, leading her out of the diner and back into the passenger seat of my car.

The feel of her body still tingles on my palms when I get into the driver side and place them on the steering wheel and gear shift.

"What else do you have in store for us today?" Why does her voice always sound like that? It makes my dick harden when I should be concentrating on the road and not crash.

"I was thinking of a walk at the park. It's a nice day today and fresh air is always good for one's soul."

"My god, you are real, aren't you?" I'm not sure if this is a good thing or bad thing. Does she not like the idea?

"I mean, we could do something else..."

Her hand on my thigh stops my mouth from continuing. I have to try hard to concentrate on breathing and not how close her fingers are to my dick.

"I'd love to take a walk with you at the park, Mat." I let out a long breath and continue to drive us safely to our next destination.

The research I did last night told me the weather would be in the seventies today. Perfect for a quick stroll. Honestly, I only thought of it because I have no fucking other idea about what to do. But I didn't want the date to end after our meal. I just wanted more time with Atsuko. The movies seemed like a bad idea because I wouldn't be able to really be with her if we're just sitting there in the dark, staring at a screen.

I felt a little too selfish for that, so a walk in the park it is.

After strolling for about a few minutes, Atsuko's hand slips into mine. The softness of her skin makes me think of how soft it would feel like holding onto my cock. Shit, I need to think unsexy thoughts before I won't be able to walk at all. That wouldn't go well.

I clear my throat and attempt again to start a conversation. That's what people do on dates, right?

"Have you lived in this area long?"

"Yeah, my parents live a couple of towns over. I left the house when I was twenty-one and never looked back. My parents are pretty independent free spirits. They didn't mind. In fact, they probably celebrated and are out partying all the time now that they're empty nesters."

"Does that mean you're an only child?"

"Oh no, I have a couple of brothers. One of them joined the military and the other is working in a different city. I don't know what he does, I just know he's doing fine living the bachelor life. I'm the baby of the family, the last to leave. We text now and again to see if the other is still alive but that's about it."

"Oh."

Not one to usually talk about my past, I try to keep the conversation about her by thinking of some more questions, but she beats me to it.

"So, do you work with Akmal full time? He said you were his personal IT guy?"

"Uh, yeah, I work with Akmal. But our normal day job is with a technical support company. It's how we met. He's the best guy I know."

"How nice. You guys seem close. Like Vero and myself. We've been friends for over a decade."

"How about you, do you model full time?"

Her laugh is beautiful.

"I wish. It would be much easier. No, as of right now, I work a makeup counter for commission. It's amazing how much money women are willing to spend on makeup. You would be surprised by the amount I bring in on a good week. Vero helps with that by hanging out when she can to boost sales with her beautiful face."

"She's not as beautiful as you."

Her eyes sparkle and her smile grows wide. She's really stunning when she smiles. I'm glad my slip of tongue didn't put my foot in my mouth. She squeezes our joined hands and takes my arm as we continue our leisurely walk around the park grounds.

Chapter Fifteen

MAT

The walk ended way too soon. The entire date ended way too soon. We're at her front door and I'm not sure what I'm supposed to do. The sites I looked up a few days ago left me conflicted on whether or not I should give her a kiss at the door. To be honest, I've never kissed anyone before and the thought alone makes my palms sweat. Miss Miller has fucked me, the women who propositioned me have fucked me. But the simple thought of kissing makes me feel like I'm about to fall to my death.

I don't know how long I stand there contemplating whether dying is worth it when Atsuko grabs the front of my shirt bringing me down and places her mouth on mine. The softness of her lips is a contrast against the strong grasp she still has on my shirt. I don't know what I'm doing but I'm lost in her touch, in her smell.

My mouth starts to pick up on her patterns quickly and soon enough a feminine sigh escapes as our tongues start to tentatively explore each other. Shit, this is almost better than sex. Who knew kissing could be this intense? Her hands leave my shirt and start to caress my face making me groan. I haven't shaved in a few days, hopefully she's not put off by my scruff.

The door behind us opens up but it doesn't stop the tongue dance we have going. I'm consumed by Atsuko's presence - fucking drowning. My mouth is getting more desperate for her by the minute, never getting enough of what she's giving me.

"I'll...uh..see you guys later. Atsuko, I'll be back tomorrow chica." I think I hear Vero leave the apartment but I'm not too sure because Atsuko grabs my shirt again and drags me into her home without taking her lips or tongue off mine, shutting the door by slamming me against it. *Holy shit.*

I make a sound of complaint when she removes her lips from mine, the sight of her smeared lipstick doing something to my insides. My cock is starting to hurt with how much it's straining behind my pants. Hours of jacking off yesterday hasn't helped me one bit.

My eyes zone in on her hand as she slowly drags the side zipper down on her dress. My hands are on the same page despite my brain being fixated on the way the bright red fabric slides to the floor revealing her beautiful naked breasts and red lace panties.

I probably broke some of the buttons in an effort to rip off my button shirt to get naked as fast as I can. I just need to feel her skin against me. I need it like my next breath.

She removes her hair tie and her dark hair cascades down like a fucking Hollywood movie. I growl under my breath and I start to take steps towards her. There's a glint in her eye as she starts to take steps back, stepping out of her heels along the way. Her eyes are raking across the expanse of my chest, arms and back to my face.

There's something inside overtaking my senses. Something primal. The farther she gets from me the more I growl in frustration because I can't smell her as much as I crave to. I need her scent on me and all over me. I'm somehow out of my pants and stalking towards her in just my boxers when I find us in a room that smells strongly of her. Her bedroom.

She turns around and looks at me over her shoulder, fuck if I don't feel my cock leak at the sight. Ever so slowly she pushes her lace panties down her legs without bending her knees whatsoever. *My god.*

When she starts crawling onto the bed, I snap and pounce on her. I've never been aggressive when it comes to sex but this girl right here does something to me. She makes me want something so fucking badly that I can't control myself.

Covering her body with mine, I flatten her onto the mattress as I rub my face all over those delicate slopes of her shoulders that have haunted my damn dreams since the first time I've seen them at the car show. My hands are greedy and they can't decide where they want to go or where they want to linger. So they're caressing everything they can reach. She's just as soft as I thought. Like a damn flower petal that a man like me shouldn't be allowed to touch and taint. Something that should have been beyond my reach.

When her ass comes up a little and grazes my erection, I hiss and kiss the shell of her ear.

"Fuck, the things you do to me."

Her breathing is deeper, a little faster.

"What do I do to you, Mat?"

"Everything. You take over my senses. I can't think straight. I can't close my eyes without seeing you."

Our lips crash again despite our awkward position while one of my hands pushes down my boxers and the other runs through her silky hair, the strands sliding through my finger-tips. I'm heating up, about to internally combust every time her tongue swipes mine. The overall temperature of the room is rising. I'm slowly getting drunk off the smell of her.

Something comes over me, making my hand grip her hair firmly, tugging her onto her back. My mouth can't get enough of her taste as I kiss, nip and suck her jaw down to her neck. *Fuck.* That little freckle by her collarbone is taunting me and so I take my time to suck even harder in retaliation to it. She grabs one of my hands and places it on her exposed breast, pushing it down, letting me know what she needs.

They're so soft, she's so damn warm. All the hours in the day wouldn't be enough for me to have my fill of her. My mouth travels lower and I envelop one of her dark nipples into my mouth like a starving man. Thoughts of my mystery girl during my lonely nights flit through my mind. Atsuko is a million times better than anything my imagination can come up with. The taste and feel of the real thing is like fucking heaven.

Not wanting her other breast to be lonely, I trail my tongue across her chest to the other nipple. If her moans and grip in my hair is anything to go by, I think I'm on the right track. My dick is telling me to hurry with the way it's forcing my hips to push against her leg. *Down boy.* I need more of a taste. I don't want this over just yet. I wonder if she tastes just as amazing between her legs? There's only one way to find out.

Peppering kisses down her belly, the smell of her arousal makes me want to cum on the fucking sheets right here. This has got to be the most beautiful pussy I have ever seen. She's nice and trim, allowing me to see her labia pinkened and puffed out. Her clit is beautiful and engorged, peeking out of its hood like it's calling me out to play. It's glistening and it makes my mouth water in anticipation of her taste. The moment my tongue touches her wetness between her folds is the moment my inner beast takes over. Licking, nipping, lapping and teasing. All those years of abuse from Miss Miller taught me how to treat a woman's pussy like a temple of worship.

"Oh my fucking god."

Nah, it's just me. Mat. And I'm fucking hungry for this. I can't stop because she tastes fucking incredible. The stiffening of her clit makes my tongue play with her even harder, kissing and teasing it like it's her mouth I'm making love to. Her body's responses only make me hotter; what she's giving me is making me feel powerful. I'm used to my dick being tortured in wait though, so she's going to have to suffer through her own form of torture with my mouth.

When her legs tighten around my head, I open my eyes to watch the look on her face. Both of her hands are squeezing and plucking at her nipples, her beautiful mouth parting as she cries out in pleasure. It's a sight I will forever sear into my memory. My tongue spears into her wet pussy as my thumb takes over where my mouth left off on her clit. I need her to give me everything she has, I deserve that reward. I've been good.

She does reward me as she rides the waves of her orgasm on my tongue, thrusting her pussy against my face in time with my tongue thrusting into her opening. My other arm pushes her legs wider in case she tries to push me off. That's not fucking happening. When the gyrations of her hips die down, I'm feeling a little put out that she only had one orgasm and so my tongue starts to thrust into her again and again a little harder. I can feel her pussy pulsating against the muscle.

"Oh my god, I can't take it. It's too much." Fuck that. She's going to take it because I need her to cum again. I fucking need it. It's for me.

Changing tactics, my mouth switches places with my hand. My fingers slowly enter her as my tongue plays with her swollen bud, nipping and sucking every now and again. Much too soon, she orgasms once more and I have to quickly maneuver my tongue in her so I can taste all of her before it escapes. It's fucking delicious and I groan against her lower lips.

Her body becomes more lax as I continue to clean up everything she's given me. My dick feels like it's going to explode with just a graze of the wind. I'm grimacing but it's a good pain. I love that I can make her feel this way, make her feel worshiped because she needs to be. She's mine to worship.

Climbing up her body, our mouths crash again and it makes me hot with how unabashedly she tastes herself on my lips. Her delicate hands graze across my chest and run down my abs making me tense up in anticipation of its destination.

She gasps into my mouth when her fingers graze across the head of my cock, making it jump in her hand like a damn pet waiting for its command. Ripping her lips from mine she looks down and gasps again.

"Holy shit. A reverse prince albert."

I've become addicted to her kisses and this little break is already killing me. She shouldn't create an addict if she isn't ready for the repercussions. Grabbing her neck, I tilt it back up where it belongs, slamming my mouth on hers with my tongue at the ready to invade her space.

Who is this man? It's me, but it's not. I've never seen this part of me before. Atsuko has opened something I don't think I will be able to close. The way she submits to everything so easily, it's a complete contradiction to every woman I've ever been with. It makes me greedy to find out everything she's willing to do.

My own fucking fantasy come to life.

The skin of my shaft is rubbing against her pussy lips back and forth, the head of my cock grazing her clit every so often. We're both breathing hard as we continue to devour each other's mouths.

"Please. Please, I need your cock in me." Has a request ever sounded so sweet? I've never once had a woman say please like she does. I can get used to this.

"Do you? Why is that?" My kisses travel to the slope of her neck again as my hips continue its torturous slide against her wet core.

"Because I feel so empty without you." Shit, it's like she's speaking to my soul. Now that I know what it's like to have her, I feel so empty just thinking about what it would be like to not have her.

Pulling my hips back, I plunge into her as deep as I can fucking go. I want to reach the depths of her soul the way she's already buried herself deep into mine. This is it. This is where I belong. This is the place my soul has been restless to find.

Atsuko's arms go around me tightly as I start to ram into her because I can't fucking help it. She feels too damn good. I don't understand why it's so different with her.

Every time it feels like I'm about to cum, I slow my hips down because I don't ever want it to end. She whimpers beneath me but I pay it no mind because I've been good. I deserve this. She brought me into her home, invited me inside of her. Just thinking about her begging me makes my dick even harder.

I don't know when my hair tie came off but my hair is falling into my eyes, slapping it every time I slap my hips against hers. The entire room smells like sex, only adding to the intoxication of the moment.

"I love the way you feel inside of me."

Shit, another thing I didn't know I was missing out on. A woman's breathless bedroom voice, whispering sweet nothings into my ear.

"I need to feel you cum inside of me. I'm on the pill."

When her tongue glides across my chest, my pounding becomes frantic. She's right. I need to feel myself cum inside of her too. This instinct to mark her as mine.

Her cries are becoming louder and louder the harder I pound into her. My abs and balls tense up, and it feels like I've been struck with electricity as I cum what feels like gallons inside of her pussy. Shouldn't masturbation reduce the amount? It feels like I've been through a long and rough dry season when it's not the case at all. The combination of our juices makes us glide against each other as the intensity of the orgasm slowly dies down. I don't want to pull out of her though, I don't want to sever the connection just yet.

Grabbing her face again in both of my hands, I place my lips gently on hers. She's my first kiss, the only person I ever want kissing me. Our mouths aren't as frantic as it started, but it's still just as sweet. My heart feels full, like the void has finally been filled to the brim and is now almost overflowing.

She tastes like fucking home.

Chapter Sixteen

ATSUKO

I've never been so worn out from sex before. I didn't even realize we fell asleep with tangled limbs until the sun came up and shone on my face waking me up. He smells of male musk and sex. This entire room does, and it makes me fucking horny. Turning my head to look at his face, he's got one arm over his eyes and the other hanging off the bed with his legs open. His decency is only covered by the corner of the sheet.

Perfect.

Slowly crawling so as to not shake the bed, I make my way south. He's beautiful to look at. The tan of his skin, the way his muscles stretch and play against the artwork across his body. The wolf on his abdomen looks like he's snarling at me but I can snarl right back.

I'll make you howl in a minute, pup.

My hands grab the corner of the sheet and slowly pull it off him like a private strip tease, revealing his defined abs and dusting of hair that points straight to the promised land.

His dick is already hard, tenting the fabric but it still does nothing to stop the small gasp that comes out of my mouth. How did I take this monster in me last night? The sun casts at just the right angle, glinting against the small curved bar on top of his penis. He's uncircumcised but the bar is small enough to fit under his foreskin, only giving a peek of what's beneath at the very head of his cock. My mouth is already watering at the memory of how it feels inside of me. I wonder what it feels like in my mouth?

Mat stirs a little, his arm still over his face, but doesn't wake up. He must be a deep sleeper. *Good.* I store that fact in the back of my mind for future reference as my hands lightly slide across his upper thighs. He has some firm quad muscles, it's impressive. No wonder his stamina's so high.

I can't take it anymore as I watch his cock twitch when I touch it with my fingers. It's like it wants to be petted but doesn't know how to ask.

That's okay boo, I got you. *Come to mama.*

I tease the firm crown of his head slowly with the tip of my tongue, running it along the underside and running it across the adornment. It makes me hot to know he's got this secret hidden away from view. Just thinking about other women knowing this about him makes me fired up with a tinge of jealousy and possessiveness.

My emotions burn with intensity as I take his entire head into my mouth, making sure my teeth don't get caught with the balls of his piercing. My tongue dances along the shaft as I take him in deeper and deeper.

His cock stretches my mouth in the most delicious way. His size matches the size of him all over. He's a big guy, but perfect for me.

The length of him almost makes me gag, but I love it. I love everything about it. My mind is imagining him fucking my face and it makes my pussy weep. Up and down, up and down, my tongue swirling on every pass around the crown of his head. He's so big, my mouth is salivating and it drips down his shaft as well as my chin, making the movement slide even more.

On one of the downward passes, I make my throat swallow, eliciting a moan from his lips. I'm getting into it, anticipating the finish when I feel a large warm hand behind my head. It only rests there, not doing anything more, making me a little frustrated at the fact. I need him wanting, I need him craving me with the same intensity in which I'm craving him. *I want to make him lose control.*

On one of the upward passes I remove my mouth from him and start licking his shaft like it's fucking melting ice cream. Nipping down the underside of his shaft all the way down, my tongue teases his ball sack, watching it tighten up with my ministrations.

Well look at that, a reaction. I love it.

My hand takes over stroking his cock where my mouth left off as I transfer my concentration to this new area. Slowly but surely sucking his sack into my mouth, my hand squeezes the crown of his cock on an upward pass. A hiss escapes him and it amps up my efforts. Moving his balls in my mouth a few times, I remove myself and return to the main attraction, his wondrous cock.

When his hand comes over the back of my head again, I moan, sending vibrations down his length, finally making him grip my hair. *Yes, just like that. I love it.*

Removing my mouth with a pop, my tongue teases his slit seductively, licking off his precum, as I open my eyes to look straight into his hooded ones. He's moved his arm to his forehead just far enough for his eyes to see everything I'm doing to him.

"I want you to fuck my face, Mat. Fuck it like you mean it."

I don't give him time to deliberate what he wants to do because I start sucking like a girl on a mission. A mission to make him give me my reward in my mouth.

My mouth is getting tired, but I don't let up. No, I need him to cum in my mouth. I need it so badly. My inner ho is crying for it.

It seems like a while before Mat gets brave enough to do what I say, and I swear I can feel my pussy clench in response, trying to grab onto empty space. *My god. I'm so fucking horny.* His hips are starting to thrust, making me gag every now and again. He's still holding back, still being too nice. But we'll get him there soon enough.

When his cock starts expanding in girth, I know I'm in the home stretch. My hand starts to fondle his balls and I give him one really good suck on the way down his shaft. The warmth of his cum shooting in my mouth does something to me. It makes me feel proud. It makes me feel like a good little girl getting her reward.

"Shit."

I take everything he has to give me, and it is a fucking lot. It starts to spill out the side of my lips despite the speed at which I'm trying to swallow. When his dick stops pulsating, and a guttural groan echoes around me, I slowly remove him from my mouth and lick the side of my lips while staring into his dark eyes. I love the way he looks when he just wakes up. I want to see it every day. I want to wake him up like this every day, worshiping his dick like he deserves.

My eyes glance back down to my hand that's still slowly stroking, and I'm surprised at what I see. He's still hard. My lady bits are getting excited at the possibilities of what this might mean for me. Could it be?

Mat's strong arms grab me and throw me onto the bed face down, lifting my hips up. His warmth comes up behind me, and he nuzzles the back of my neck. He enters me in the slowest of motions, torturing my already sensitive pussy in the best of ways. I'm so wet that he just glides in and out leisurely, as his lips kiss a trail across my shoulder blade.

"You're so fucking beautiful it hurts, Atsuko."

The stuff that comes out of his mouth just can't be real.

His dick starts to increase in speed and my ass starts to back up in time with it. I want him. I want him so bad. My pussy is starting to clench and the bitch loves the big dick it's clenching around.

The wet sound of our bodies slapping is doing something to me.

Thump thump thump.

"Keep that shit down, I'm trying to sleep!"

His masculine chuckle against my spine sends shivers down my body straight to my core. I love the way he feels so comfortable with me right now. Like he's a whole different person from the man I met the first time. *I did that.*

His hand suddenly pushes my neck from behind, shoving my face into the mattress every time his thrust becomes harder and harder. Despite the muffled message from the other side of the wall, my cries start to become louder and louder every time he buries himself in me to the hilt.

His speed picks up like he's a fucking beast, the pleasure teetering onto the point of delicious pain from the friction until he groans again and buries himself one last time. I can literally feel his cock pulsating inside of me and it's empowering. A goddess's potion.

He keeps my hips up as the hand that was behind my neck travels to the front of me right onto my clit. The man plays me like an instrument, slowly rocking his softening cock inside of me until a climax takes over and I see stars behind my eyelids. *Holy shit.* I've never felt so satiated like this, ever.

Mat might just be the man to kill me through sex... but what a way to go.

Chapter Seventeen

MAT

"I take it that the date went well?" Akmal has a goofy expression on his face, and you know what? I probably do too. I feel like I'm on fucking cloud nine.

My sack feels lighter, that's for sure. Atsuko is just as insatiable as I am. Who knew? Thinking about anyone else knowing that fact about her makes me feel uneasy. I really need to rein in my temper around her.

"I've never seen you late to work ever. You barely made it with like a minute to spare."

"Well, I made it. I had to take care of my girl. Vero kicked us out because she couldn't sleep, so she spent Sunday with me."

"Shooo! From one date to spending the night? Damn man, I'm going to need you to give me some pointers."

"Shit, I have no fucking idea what I'm doing. It just feels like once we start, we can't keep our hands off each other." I want my hands on her right now.

"Life goals, man." Akmal looks like he really is contemplating his life at the moment. How did my life turn around like this? One day I'm just an IT guy helping a buddy out, the next I'm in a whirlwind of a relationship.

I have no regrets. It's the best thing that's happened to my life so far.

"Boys, quit messing around. We got calls lining up." Tricia's voice brings me out of my Sunday reverie and I start grabbing my tools before heading out to the designated work vehicle. I wonder if she made it to work alright.

"Shit, I only wish I was so lucky." I am a lucky bastard, aren't I?

"I forgot to tell you, Vero wants your number. She mentioned it before I took Atsuko out. Sorry, it slipped my mind all weekend."

Akmal is throwing punches in the air and bouncing on his feet causing the other employees to look at us. I'm laughing because I really don't give a rat's ass about this place anymore. Akmal and I both are going to put in our two-week notice soon.

"Akmal, you got this order." Tricia hands him the written telephone order and then turns to me, the octaves of her voice getting a little lower. "Hey you, Miss Miller is requesting you again."

My day just went sour.

"Pass her to Travis. He's familiar with her cases." Tricia's face has an expression I can't read but it disappears quickly so I pay it no mind. I'm still feeling the high of last weekend.

"Travis! You got an order!" Without taking her eyes off me, she hands me the work order that's under Miss Miller's case without another word.

Good. Now my day is looking up again. Atsuko is good for me. I'm feeling on top of the world.

I handle the morning's caseload pretty quickly and soon enough, it's lunch time. Akmal is just putting his tools away when I hear Tricia speaking to someone behind me.

"We're about to close for lunch break, you'll have to come back later."

"Oh, I was hoping to catch Mat. He hasn't left yet, has he?" I know that voice anywhere. It's been whispering in my ear in the heat of the moment.

"Does he know you?" I've never heard Tricia sound like *that* before. It's kind of ticking me off, how she's speaking to my girl.

Walking back towards the direction of the front desk quickly before anything else happens, Atsuko's eyes and face lights up when she sees me. It feels like my heart is being squeezed. Damn, a man can get used to that kind of welcome.

"Hey, beautiful." I don't have any more words to give her because my mind is on one track right now, to touch her as fast as possible.

I do just that when I reach her, placing my arms behind the small of her back and bending her back to kiss the lips I've been missing all day.

"Give them some privacy Tricia." I don't know what she's doing and I don't care. My entire being is zoned in on this woman in my arms. *My woman.*

Atsuko moans a little as our tongues tangle, her hands running through my hair, probably losing my hair tie again. Shit, I can feel my dick stirring and trying to home in on her hot center.

Using what strength I have, I pull my mouth from hers and caress her delicate nose with my own.

"Have lunch with me." Her smile is blinding no matter how many times I've been privileged to see it and it makes my heart stutter.

"Of course. I missed you." Her hooded eyes make me want to eat *her* for lunch.

"Good because I missed you too." I should just leash her to my side. Would that be too much?

"Uh.. should I do lunch solo then?" I can barely register Akmal's voice as I continue to stare into her eyes.

"Hell no, you're not. Excuse me chica, I'm going to have to ask you to stop staring at my BFF with her man. It's kind of rude. Akmal, you're not bailing on me, are you?"

"I ... uh, I didn't even know you were here."

"That's because you forgot to ask me for my number. I came to make sure you never forget it again."

"Holy shit." I chuckle as I hear Akmal's voice under his breath.

"So, who's driving?" I can already see Vero dragging Akmal out the front door in my periphery as I give Atsuko another kiss on the lips.

"Tricia, we'll be back in an hour." Clearing my throat, I straighten my woman back up without removing my hands from her.

I don't hear what she mumbles as Atsuko and I leave right behind Akmal and Vero.

We eat at Sammi's, and with the addition of Vero, conversations go a little smoother. For me and Akmal anyway. Vero can talk anyone's ear off.

"So Mat, where are you from?"

"Uh.. originally Montana. I was living on one of the reservations." It's been a while since I stepped foot in that state. I drove as far as my car would take me after leaving.

Atsuko's face brightens at that tidbit. I really don't like talking about my past. I don't want her to know of the dark stain that's on my soul. Surprisingly, she isn't pushing for more.

"Oh, I see. So does that mean you have a tribe? Is that what they call it? I'm sorry if I'm prying." Vero doesn't look sorry at all, but she also doesn't look like she means anything malicious by her statement. I can't blame her curiosity, at least she has the decency to ask and not assume.

"Blackfoot Indian."

"Does that mean you have an Indian name?" Atsuko's question is soft, probably to let me know that I don't have to answer if I don't want to. When she's like this, I want to do whatever she wants.

"Matunaagd Big Crow. But Mat is fine." A smile creeps up on her lips but Atsuko doesn't say anything else. There's a calm about her that I enjoy. My soul feeds on it, always wanting to be around her so that it can rub off on me.

"Does your name mean anything?" It's my turn to ask her. I find myself falling deep into her eyes. It feels like no one exists at this moment but her, here, now.

"My parents are second-generation Japanese American. From what I've been told, Atsuko means honest and sincere while my last name Kobayashi means small forest." I take in everything she tells me like it's gold. Small forest, huh? Is this where my soul was longing to roam? This can't be a coincidence, can it?

"Akmal..." Vero's voice is practically purring like a kitten towards him. She is not shy about showing her interest at all. That's one thing I noticed about these two women. They are full of life and confidence.

"What does your name mean?" She puts her hand on her chin and leans in closer while Akmal subtly leans a little farther back in his chair.

I stifle a laugh when he tries to clear his throat and keep a friendly smile on his face before he answers her. Vero has a really strong energy and it can be overwhelming to be around.

"Blessed clever son of an intelligent mind. Or something like that."

"Ohh... clever and intelligent. Just the way I like them. Perfect, really."

Her finger touches his thigh and Akmal almost falls off his chair. The girls laugh and Akmal gives us all a sheepish look when he straightens back up and takes a big sip of his water. This poor guy's got it bad and he can't do a thing about it.

Chapter Eighteen

MAT

Akmal and I put in our two-week notice at the same time. Morty was dumbfounded when he saw us come into his office together, but it serves him right. He's always thinking everything under his control is going fine and dandy when in reality, not many of us are happy with the way things are. A great leader makes a big difference, and Morty is always hiding himself away in his office leaving the peons to pick up all the slack. Some days I wonder if I'm really the only one with a Miss Miller problem.

It's only been a month since the car show, but all the time Atsuko and I have been spending together never seems to be enough. My craving for her is only getting stronger and stronger, making me question whether my obsession with her is even healthy.

Akmal and Vero still haven't gone on an actual date yet, but she's been coming by the job often to eat lunch with him.

Akmal is a harder guy to catch despite how friendly he is. He's not used to all the attention and Vero kind of scares him with her personality. I'm kind of scared for him myself. His culture also doesn't let him get too close to a woman before marriage, let alone touch them in more than a friendly manner. Vero's got her hands full if she wants to catch Akmal.

Atsuko has been spending half her weeks with me at my place and it kills me every time she goes back to her apartment. I shouldn't be this greedy, I should appreciate whatever she gives me but damn if I don't want to just lock her up in my bedroom and throw away the key.

Every time I walk her to her front door, her male neighbors are always hanging around. It's like they know her schedule and fucking hang out in packs waiting for my female to return to her damn den. I try to get a handle on my rage by signing up for an MMA gym to get some of my aggression out on the heavy bags.

But today is not going to be one of my best days.

Atsuko is just about to insert her key into her door when the hairs on the back of my neck rise. The sound of male voices are getting louder and louder and my head is starting to feel tight, making my teeth grind. They sound drunk and rowdy. I hate rowdy crowds.

My girl shouldn't be subject to living next to this shit.

"Hey, baby! Haven't seen you around in a while. Where have you been giving tail? I want some of that."

My mind is in a red haze and I can't see anything but his neck and eyes as they start to become bloodshot from my hands squeezing tighter and tighter. I don't even know how I ended up on top of him, pushing his skull into the ground in time with my choking the life out of him. Hands and limbs are trying to pull me off which only makes me angrier. Releasing one of my hands, I elbow the face behind me before I start pummeling this fucker's nose in so he can stop sniffing around my girl. The impact of my knuckles and the sound of the crunch makes me smile as I continue to throw blow after blow. My fists start to slip with the blood that's starting to seep out.

This fucker has been after my girl every single time I bring her back to her apartment. All these stupid frat boys and their drinking parties, hanging out like stray dogs sniffing up the wrong fucking female. *My female.*

The smell of hard liquor burning my nostrils starts to flash my mind back to the past and my body goes on autopilot. Male grunts, the sound of flesh hitting walls, the tinkling of broken glass, the shattering of broken bottles, the metallic smell mixing in with the alcohol. It all becomes a blur.

It only feels like a second in time but I know it's been longer. I'm standing over a pile of bodies that are moaning and rolling on the ground. Some blood is splattered in areas, some faces are unrecognizable and smeared in crimson.

When the red haze slowly lifts from my mind's eye, I take a few steps back causing the broken glass under my boots to crunch. My breath is heaving, the blood flow in my veins making me feel hot all over. There's tension in my shoulder muscles and I still feel the adrenaline coursing through me.

When none of the boys on the ground speak anything coherent, I slowly turn my gaze behind me. Atsuko's eyes are wide. There's fear but there's also concern in her gaze. Shit, what did I do?

"You are your father's son. We share the same blood. So don't look at me like you're better than me because you aren't. Just wait and see, boy."

No, I'm not my father. I'll never be him. My inner demons are trying to lie to me again, trying to play their tricks on my mind.

I can feel my teeth grind down again when the sting and throb starts to register in my fists and elbows. Fuck, I can't believe I lost control like that. In front of Atsuko of all people. What must she think of me?

"...I..." I fucked things up, didn't I?

Atsuko walks towards me slowly like I'm an injured animal about to make a break for it. To be honest, that's exactly how I feel and it's exactly what I'm contemplating.

When her hands cradle my face in her warmth, my eyes close in resignation knowing what's coming. It was heaven while it lasted but a man like me never deserved her. A man like me never deserved to even have that little slice of heaven I was given.

———

ATSUKO

What just happened?

I knew these guys were going to get their asses handed to them one of these days. Cocky young guys always do, or else they never learn. It's a good thing I blocked Alfonso's number because he would have been trouble too.

I just didn't think it would be my sweet Mat to do it. I never knew he had this side of him. He's never given me any indication of anything other than being a shy and genuine person when he's around me.

When his body straightened up to his full height and the tension in his shoulders started stiffening, was the moment I knew something was going to happen. Something big. I would never be able to hold him back even on my best day. Mat is a big guy even though he never throws it around.

But today. Today was the day I saw a beast emerge from its cage. It was like watching a train wreck in slow motion except everything happened so damn fast. All I saw were bodies being thrown, limbs moving and the sound of Mat rearranging the poor boy's face.

I should be appalled.

Alfonso has this temper.

I should be upset.

But Alfonso is never in the right when he goes ballistic. He's usually the instigator of problems.

I shouldn't be so turned on with all the blood he's shedding in my name.

Mat's body is all lethal grace even when he's erupting in fury. A controlled chaos.

And I've had all that potential power and energy down on his knees between my legs, worshiping me like I'm the most delicate thing he's ever had privy to hold.

My poor baby has so many facets to him, depths I haven't seen and it just draws the curious pussycat in me even more. Cradling his face between my hands, I can't help but feel my heart break with the look of resignation I see there. What's going on in that mind of his?

"Mat."

His eyes are still closed, worry lines appearing on his forehead and I can feel a sense of sorrow radiating off him in waves.

"Mat, look at me please."

I can tell he's fighting with himself about something. There's an internal battle I'm not invited to. My eyes are glued to the way his dark lashes fan across his high cheekbones, memorizing the slopes of his features. Mat sighs and finally opens his eyes, his dark irises staring into my soul with a question I'm not sure I understand.

The groans on the ground remind me that we're still outside of my apartment.

I give him a soft kiss on the lips before grasping his hand in mine and leading him inside, making sure to lock the door behind us.

Chapter Nineteen

ATSUKO

Leading Mat to our small couch, I urge him to sit down while I go find the first aid kit. He doesn't look like he took too much damage versus the other guys, but it's still good to give him a once over anyway. The good thing about Vero being my roommate is that we're both pretty organized. Things are quickly and easily found.

When I return from the restroom, Mat has his head in his hands, elbows on his knees. My heart hurts all over again at the sight before me. I've never seen him look so defeated.

Slowly getting on my knees before him, I put my hand on his shoulder and place the first aid kit on the floor beside me. His knuckles are bleeding but it doesn't look to be bothering him one bit. His breathing is slow and even, the muscles of his forearms flexing every now and again. He isn't moving besides that and I'm starting to get worried. Taking a chance,

I slowly get to my feet and wrap my arms around him in a hug despite him continuing to sit leaning forward.

"Mat, baby. It's okay. I'm here. I'm not going anywhere, alright?"

He groans and turns his body to bury his face in my chest, arms wrapping tightly around me like he's afraid I'll leave him, as I sit my butt down onto the couch beside him.

"I don't deserve you. You must hate me." I can barely hear his whispers since he's essentially talking to the top of my breasts but I slowly rub his back until I start to feel some of the tension leave his body.

The room is quiet except for the sound of our mutual breathing. I was able to maneuver my body so that at least half of me is lying down on the couch with Mat right on top of me, still holding onto me for comfort. *My poor baby.*

With my head on the armrest of the couch, I start to just spew out the first thing off the top of my head.

"You know, I didn't grow up in the best of neighborhoods. One of the girls on my street, who had it out for me, was following me from work while I was walking home."

My hands continue to caress his back in slow patterns as Mat starts to settle into the crook of my neck, his warm breath fanning my cleavage. I take a deep breath through my nose, taking in the unique smell of Mat. *My man.* There's a hint of copper today, probably from the blood.

"I knew what she was up to, so I took a detour. She followed me of course, because she thought she had me. About a house or two from my destination, I ran. She tried to take me down but I turned around just in time to throw the first punch, knocking her to her ass. Vero came barreling out of her house and we were both ready for her to get back up." I chuckle as I remember my BFF and I together. It was before any of us had a car. You can try to take the girl off the streets, but you can't truly take the streets out of the girl. It becomes a part of you, a dark splotch inside of you that can never really be washed away. We are the sum of all of our parts.

"She tried of course, but we took her down. She never followed me home again. Seems she had it out for me because the guy she liked was hanging out around the coffee shop I worked at too often."

I kiss the top of Mat's head and run my hands through his hair.

"There will always be outside forces that work against us, even if we try our best to mind our business and just live our life."

I caress his exposed cheek and urge him to come closer to my face, which he complies. Our kiss is slow, steady, a reaffirmation perhaps. Our tongues enter each other's mouths like a lover's embrace, our lips keeping it soft and subtle like we're making love through our kiss alone.

Making him pull away from our kiss with my hands on his cheeks, I look deeply into his eyes watching to see if the sorrow is still there. He watches me back just as intently, panting lightly through his parted lips.

"I see you, Mat." My eyes roam his face from his brows, to his dark eyes, to his clean shaven face today, to his strong nose and back to his full lips. My fingers move his escaped locks of hair from his eye and caress his ear. "You're all I see."

His kisses become desperate and needy. They're searching for something, and I don't know what it is. I only hope that I can give him what he needs from me. I feel like I'm drowning in his transferred emotions when he pulls away from me ever so slightly, both of our lips parted only millimeters away from each other, the warmth of our breaths still close enough to mingle between us.

"I don't understand why you would even want to be with someone like me, let alone after today. I don't deserve you, and yet it feels like my heart is being ripped out of my chest at just the thought of being without you." Despite his jarring words, his lips start to travel down towards my cleavage. One of his hands roughly pulls down my shirt and bra, exposing my breast to his warm mouth. Mat is a master at worshiping every part of me. He's wrong. I probably don't deserve someone like him.

Suddenly, our hands are clawing at one another, trying to rip each other's clothes off as fast as we can. Once we're able to get the essential pieces off, Mat's already slamming his hard dick home with one of my legs over his shoulder making him feel even deeper than before. Mat is a man who knows how to work what God has blessed him with. But it's really the passion behind everything he does that takes sex to a whole other level.

The sound of the door opening almost doesn't register amidst the grunts and cries we're making on the couch. We're both drowning in each other, chasing that elusive cliff, wanting to free dive off it together.

"What the fuck happened out there?...oh..."

We don't hear from Vero again until Mat purges all his frustrations out on my pussy a few more times that night.

Chapter Twenty

MAT

Atsuko and I have become closer since that day I lost my control. I don't know how she does it, but she calms me. I'm not a perfect man by any means, God knows I don't come from perfect stock either. Hopefully, she never has to find out about my past misdeeds, the stain on my soul. She's the bright light to my darkness. Shit, I don't deserve her but I can't fucking let her go.

I was able to convince her to stay at my place at least four days out of the seven. I'll take anything she'll give me. Honestly, I need to start figuring out how to make her permanently move in without seeming like a creep.

When she's not around, my dick is getting abused by my hand constantly and it still isn't enough. It's nowhere close to being the same when I'm buried inside of her warmth, being held in her arms. How can such a small person bring me happily to my knees?

"Mat, what's going on man?"

"I'm trying to figure out how to keep Atsuko at my house permanently."

Akmal laughs like it's the funniest shit ever, when I'm fucking serious as hell.

"Nah man, I'm not laughing at you. I'm laughing because you look fucking serious as all get out. You guys are intense. Has she mentioned anything about it?"

"I mean, she's at my place half the week anyway. What difference does it make if she stays the whole week...and just never goes back? I can take her to work, do whatever she wants me to do."

"I guess it really isn't that different. What does Vero think about that? I mean, they're best friends and all."

"She never crossed my mind. Maybe I'll just keep myself between her legs until she can't say no. Eat her out until she doesn't want to go home."

"I mean, that sounds like it could work. I wouldn't know, since I've never done it. But it sounds legit."

I'm contemplating when to put this plan into action when the sound of a voice I have been avoiding floats into the air of the building. *It can't be.*

"There you are. Why haven't you been taking my cases? I've been requesting for you for what feels like over a month and a half."

Miss Miller is standing at the front desk, staring at me. I almost don't recognize her because I've only ever seen her with a robe and hair bun and not normal street clothes. Where the hell is Tricia? I know for damn sure she's on today, I saw her this morning.

"Akmal, where is Travis?"

"Shit, let me go look for him."

"Miss Miller, I'm going to have to ask you to take a seat while I find someone who can help you."

The front door opens but I can't remove my eyes from her because she's that damn predator that takes anything as a challenge. I can't back down from this one. Not now. It's been too good, I knew something was bound to happen sooner or later.

I hear Akmal talking to who I hope is Travis in one of the rooms nearby.

"No, I'm not going to have a seat because I want you to come back to my house, to me. I want things to go back to the way they were. I miss you. I miss you between my legs."

"What. The. Fuck. Did. You. Say?" Shit, the person who came in was Atsuko. She was so quiet during her entrance, I didn't even know if it was a woman or man who entered.

"Excuse me little girl, I'm trying to have a conversation with my man right now. You're going to have to just wait your turn."

"The fuck? I think you are mistaken *ma'am*, because you are talking to *my* man right now who is about to go on his lunch break with *me*."

"Oh honey, he's just toying with you. I'll always be his one and only. His *first* and only." Shit. I don't know why my words are stuck in my throat. I feel like punching something, but I'm still on duty with a few more hours of my day to go.

Miss Miller leans towards Atsuko and I'm already walking around the counter to stop this nonsense she's spewing.

"He always comes back home to mama, with his head between my legs. If you think I'm lying, let me tell you that that piercing on his dick was for *me*."

Atsuko's fist collides into Miss Miller's face with a loud *thwack* before I can make it in time, landing the poor woman on the floor. I can see Travis from the corner of my eye, seeing to her sprawled body and sobs as I grab Atsuko by the waist and lift her off the floor to prevent her from dealing out any more damage than necessary. Atsuko is seething in silence, but her face is contorted in utter rage. She's kicking, trying to jump out of my arms, and I'm surprised I'm able to bring her safely out of the building through the back entrance by the employee parking lot.

When I place her feet back down on the ground, she's throwing punches at my chest. What the fuck did I do?

"Were you seeing her behind my back? She took your virginity, right? That's what she was fucking saying? Are you still hung up on her because she was your first?"

She's out of her fucking mind. Miss Miller is nothing to me. Nothing but an evil ball and chain that refuses to let me leave and live my life in peace. My mind is racing with everything I want to say but my mouth can't catch on to what I should say first. I must look like a dying fish with my mouth opening and closing without actually talking.

"I knew it was too good to be true. You were too good to be true...to want just me. What does she have that I don't, Mat? Is there something I'm missing? Am I not enough for you?"

Watching her eyes tear up makes me snarl and growl into the air. Fuck, I suck at this shit. The anger inside of me, the humiliation, the suddenness of it all is making me tongue tied, and I'm fucking it up even more by not saying the right things to fix it.

"It's not what it fucking looks like."

"Yeah? What does it look like to you Mat? Because to me..." She's crying. The tears she was holding back are falling down her face and I feel like a fucking piece of shit for causing it. I want to claw my eyes out so I don't have to watch her tortured expression before me. Am I as bad as my father? Is my blood that tainted in darkness that I end up hurting my woman like this? I feel like everything is going out of fucking control with each tear that falls down her precious face.

She's losing her voice through her sobs and hiccups. "...Because to me, I don't know Mat. But it fucking hurts. It *hurts* so fucking much." She covers her face in her hands and runs away from me. Like that, I feel worse than a piece of shit. I feel like nothing. I did that to her. She should never have to cry because of me.

Fuck!

The sound of her car screeching away makes me feel like acid is burning beneath my skin. I can't catch my breath, what the fuck do I do? How do I fix this? I'm not cut out for this relationship shit and I should have known it was going to end up this way. I never deserved her.

My body squats down and my head is in my hands. I feel like pulling my damn hair out as I growl once more towards the ground beneath me.

"Shit, what happened?" Akmal's voice is barely registering. All I can hear is the woosh and roar of my heartbeat next to my ears. My head feels like it's stuffed with cotton. My heart. Fuck, my heart feels like it's been ground under a large boot, singed by fire and smeared back into the Earth as ash.

Chapter Twenty-One

ATSUKO

My heart hurts. It feels like it's been shattered into a million pieces. The way it scrapes my insides even though there are no physical wounds.

I don't know what to believe because, I know Mat feels deeply for me. But what that woman said slithers into my mind like poison, infecting anything I believe, everything I thought I believed. I know it shouldn't let it, but it does.

"I'll always be his one and only. His first and only."

It echoes in my mind like a damn chant, beating me down a little piece at a time when I *know* I'm not stupid enough to believe it...but it still fucking hurts to hear it. My insecurities and doubts start to overtake my mind like vines on a deserted building.

Mat didn't say anything at all. What does it mean? Does he agree? Was he just trying to let me down easy? After all we've been through together? Was it all just one-sided? Was I the only one feeling the deep connection between us? Was it only for the sex? He should have said that up front if that was the case, and this wouldn't hurt so bad.

It never hurt this much the first time Alfonso and I broke up. But then again, I've never felt this deeply about someone before.

I never told him...but I was falling in love with Mat. Heart, mind and soul.

The way that woman spoke of Mat's cock like she's been so intimate with it for so damn long - It speared me, ripping out my heart to watch it die a slow death.

Was what she said true? He's been with me almost every day since we've been together. *Almost.* What does he do on those other days? Does he run back to her?

She came to his place of work. Does he go back to her while on duty? Is that how they met? Again, where does that leave me? Who am I? Am I the side piece?

...Is this why he always says he doesn't deserve me? Was he admitting to something and I just wasn't smart enough to catch the clues?

Just thinking about it makes my chest ache. These tears won't stop falling and I can't even speak straight to explain to Vero what happened.

I should be too old for this, shouldn't I? Isn't this what teenagers do? I can't fucking help it. I can't stop the way I feel. Mat was my reason for waking up, what made me smile before I went to sleep. I was thinking about maybe bringing up the idea of us living together when I walked into that shit show yesterday - just to watch it all burn down into ashes. All it took was one kindle, one flame to tear everything my heart has built up.

I'm in Vero's arms and she's rocking me, giving me tender kisses on the forehead as we both sit here on my bed. I feel so pathetic. Damn my heart for loving a man like Mat.

"Okay, try to catch your breath chica. I'm not sure I'm getting the story right." That makes me sob even harder and hiccup into her chest because dammit, it feels like it just happened a minute ago even though it's already the next morning. My words catch in my throat, unable to relay how my heart was torn again. Shaking my head side to side, my forehead scraping against her shirt roughly - I just can't. My eyes burn too damn much, these stupid hiccups wont let me talk straight or gather my thoughts corrrectly.

"It's okay. It's okay."

She took a few days off work, calling into my job as well, to be here with me while I wallow in my self pity party. Because really, isn't that what this is?

My body slinks down to the side on my bed and Vero comes with me, still holding me from behind for comfort. I must have fallen asleep because when I open up my swollen eyes, my room is dark and Vero is nowhere to be seen. With no motivation to even move, I just close my eyes again hoping for the darkness to consume me quickly so I don't have to feel anything anymore.

VERO

What the fuck happened? I've never seen Atsuko like this. She's has a trail of men left in her wake trying to catch any scraps she might give out. She's the one usually dolling out heartache, not receiving it - She's never cried like someone just fucking died right in front of her. I hope no one died. I don't *think* anyone died.

I'm sitting in front of her closed bedroom door sitting on the ground with my head back, listening to her breathing slow back down, letting me know she went back to sleep. My heart aches in echo to hers from listening to her own heartache seeping out of her very pores. Closing my eyes all I can see is her puffed out eyes and pain - I feel so damn helpless! I feel like punching someone but I don't know who I should punch! She hasn't eaten anything all day, only taking small sips of water since I've been leaving random bottles in her room. Her hiccuping sobs were making my chest hurt. Holding back my own tears for her was hard because I didn't want to add to it. I wanted to be strong for her.

Slowly getting to my feet, I stretch out my kinks and go to the living room to get my phone. Sitting my tired ass on the couch, my fingers start flying across the keyboard.

Vero : what the fuck happened between Mat and Atsuko yesterday?

Akmal : I'm not really sure. One of our clients showed up out of the blue.

Vero: what the hell does that have to do with anything?

Akmal : It's a long story.

Fuck this shit. Someone needs to tell me *something* because Atsuko's story was so fragmented, nothing made any damn sense.

Dialing his number, I put the phone to my ear. Fucker better pick up if he knows what's good for him.

"...Hello."

I'm whisper-yelling through the phone's microphone, not wanting to wake Atsuko. "Akmal! Tell me what happened, right now! I don't know how to help Atsuko if I don't know the full story."

"...I..I'm not sure myself."

"Tell me what you *do* know. You know more than I do because you were at least there."

I listen intently to everything Akmal is telling me. My heart is breaking for Atsuko all over again because I can see where she's coming from. The question remains with what happened between the two love birds in the back parking lot though. According to Akmal, Mat was already reverted into a shell of despair and rage by the time he arrived on the scene and Atsuko was already long gone.

Chapter Twenty-Two

MAT

There was at least a week left on the two weeks notice we put in. But I couldn't go back to work after the crap show with Miss Miller. That sorry excuse for an IT company is a dark stain on my mind.

I couldn't go back to my place either, too many memories of her. My bedroom alone smells like her, making the cavern in my chest open even wider. Life isn't the same. Home isn't where my heart is anymore. My heart drove away as I felt myself crumble into dust.

Akmal was nice enough to let me crash at his place. This is going to be his last day with Morty, because he said he only stuck around to be with me anyway. *Fuck that place.*

I don't know what kind of company I'm going to be for him, feeling like a shell of myself. I don't have any motivation to do anything but wallow in the sorrow that's consuming me. All this time alone is dangerous for my mind because not only do I constantly have thoughts of what could have been with Atsuko, my failures, thoughts of the past start creeping up again. Like it was just waiting for a chance to eat at my soul when I'm in a weakened state. And I feel fucking weak right now.

Have I eaten today? Fuck, I need to punch something.

Getting off Akmal's couch, I grab the duffel bag I took from my place and change into workout gear. The movements of my body slow as I walk out of Akmal's home and lock the door behind me. The drive to the gym is a quiet one, the music in the car doing nothing to calm me, instead only sounding like TV static in the background no matter how many times I change songs.

When I get to the gym, there's already a small handful of guys there. I pay them no mind as I walk towards the item that's going to receive all of my frustrations. *Thwack thwack.* From the side, the front, more shoulder power. What frustration I came in with has now increased tenfold. *Thwack Thwack Thwack Thwack.* I'm sweating like a beast, my wet hair slapping my face as I continue to pound into the heavy bag in front of me. Sometimes I imagine it being Miss Miller's face because I would never hurt a woman in real life. But in my anger and rage, this red heavy bag makes me think of Miss Miller's red hair. My knuckles are starting to get sore but it doesn't stop me at all. The clinking of the chains that hold the heavy bag up is turning into a melody that slowly soothes my hurt soul.

With a snarl and growl, I throw my last few punches with as much force as I can, making the heavy bag swing in a wide arc. Grabbing my hair, I turn and feel like ripping it out again but hold myself back. FUCK! I'm in public, and I probably already look like a raging beast about to blow a gasket and devour the crowd already here. A few of the people are looking at me discreetly from their workouts, but no one dares to say anything.

Grabbing the towel from the back pocket of my shorts, I wipe off my face and contemplate my life. All the shit I've gone through thus far...just to be in *more* shit? In *more* of a mess? This can't possibly be my destiny. What was I put on this earth for? Everything good in my life gets taken away. It's worse when I'm given a taste of how good it can be. I fucking laugh like a lunatic. Matunaagd: *He who fights.* Big Crow: *aren't crows a symbol of death anyway?* I must have always been destined to forever fight something until the day I die.

This must be part of the torture, right? It wouldn't hurt so bad if I didn't have a taste at all. I should probably just give up on finding anyone. No one compares to Atsuko anyway. There's no woman in the world that would live up to what I now know - of what it could have been between us. A slice of heaven down here in this hell we call life.

After showering, I walk out of the gym towards my car, my thoughts still morose. The heavy bag was only a temporary fix.

My mind for some reason drifts to the men in Atsuko's building and to Atsuko's ex. Fucking hell. They're probably chomping at the bit already when they realize I'm not coming around. I'm pissed all over again but more so about the fact that I now have no right to beat them to the ground. I should fucking do it anyway to make myself feel better.

"Mat? Is that you?" I'm still brooding over the many ways I can kill a man and get away with it before I realize I recognize the feminine voice.

"Tricia? What are you doing here?"

"...I, uh, I just signed up. What are the odds we'd have the same gym, right?"

"I guess."

There's an awkward silence between us and I'm getting agitated because my mind hasn't come up with ways to stay out of a hypothetical jail yet after I kill every male that sniffs around Atsuko.

"Hey, I heard about what happened the other day."

What happened? She makes it sound like a mere incident report instead of the crashing and decimation of my whole fucking world.

"You know, if you ever need anything. I'm here for you. Even if it's just...to work out frustrations." What the hell is she talking about? I was just working out my frustrations on the heavy bag, not like it fucking helped any. I don't know her reasons for signing up for this particular gym and I really don't care.

"Yeah."

I start walking to my car again, my mind still full of morbid thoughts, when the feeling of someone's hands on my bicep stops me.

"I'm down for a quickie if you need it. As friends, of course. Just trying to help a friend out. I mean, you're a guy and I'm a girl. I can help you scratch an itch if you need it." She bites her bottom lip and it reminds me of Atsuko. The way her eyes would get hooded and her lips would part when my head is between her legs, worshiping her for hours. I fucking miss her even more and my heart is hurting all over again at my loss, the wound ripping open like it's the first time. Trying to think of anything else to balm the hurt, I think of everything that happened that day.

"Where were you that day, Tricia? I could have sworn you were on duty. But when Miss Miller came by, you were nowhere to be seen. How the hell did Miss Miller know to come in at that time anyway? She never comes in."

Something crosses her features. The adrenaline from my workout hasn't gone down all the way yet and so my senses are still heightened. What the hell was that? A sick feeling enters my gut and my mind is quickly starting to piece something together.

But it doesn't make any sense. Does it? Why would she?

"Where were you, Tricia?" I'm not one to be this way. To be out of control with my temper. But losing Atsuko did something to me. It unleashed a beast, and the beast just sniffed a trail of deceit.

"I..I must have been in the restroom or something."

"Then how did you know about what happened? I never came back to work and Akmal isn't a talker when it comes to my business. You handle the calls, so how would Miss Miller know that I've been purposely avoiding her?" I mean, Miss Miller could have taken a good guess but something is just not sitting right.

I'm looking at all of Tricia's features with suspicion, when I see her face change from innocent to angry. What the fuck is happening right now?

"You were fucking mine. I saw you before that Asian bitch ever did, you know that? I was handling Miss Miller, figuring out how to permanently get her away from you, and what do I have to show for all my hard work? Losing you to someone who slid in when the opportunity arose. An opportunity I created, because I always had your back, Mat!"

Come again? Am I in the fucking Twilight Zone right now? The way she's raising her voice at me is triggering something inside and it's pissing me off. What the fuck did *I* do? Trying to calm my nerves, I take a deep breath in and out before I speak.

"Tricia, I have no idea what you are talking about. I appreciate everything you did for me with Miss Miller. Travis was handling things on his end as well."

"Travis? Ha! That fucker is lucky he hasn't been written up. Miss Miller has been sending in complaint cards on him and it was *me* who kept trashing them so the arrangement could continue. I mean, I don't blame the old woman. I've been trying to get a piece of you too but you are just too damn hard headed to see it."

I must have not eaten enough today because nothing is making any damn sense. My head must not be hearing things correctly, my brain synapses aren't firing right.

"I have no idea what the fuck you are talking about, Tricia. I never sensed any interest from you, besides being friendly at work."

"And this is exactly why there is a trail of hearts behind you, Mat. You're too fucking perfect." She takes an exaggerated deep breath. "Let's just stop fighting, alright. Come on, let's go back to my car and I'll suck your cock. Would you like that? I'll make you feel good and help you forget all the crap that's happened."

How in the world did we get from redirecting client cases to her asking to suck my dick?

"I don't think that's a good idea, Tricia. Sorry, but it's going to be a no."

Trying to escape this beyond awkward situation, I take quick strides to my vehicle. I'm about to unlock my car when Tricia turns me and slams me into the driver's side door. *What the hell?* My eyes widen when she lowers herself and starts fumbling with the buttons of my pants. I have to force her hands and body away from me with a firm grip on both of her wrists.

"Tricia, I said no."

"I heard what Miss Miller said about your cock, Mat. I want that pierced dick in my mouth, please!" *What the hell?* That means Tricia *was* standing in that office the entire time the shit show happened...and *let it* happen.

Wait.

"Fucking hell, Tricia? Did you set that shit up?" Tell me it isn't so. Fuck.

"If I say, yes will you let me go down on you? Fuck, Mat. I don't know how else I can tell you how much I want to be with you. It's always been you. That girl got in the way. I had to end it. I had to, you have to see that I did it for *us*."

This girl is out of her fucking mind. If I was the person I was before meeting Atsuko, I might have fallen for this shit. But Atsuko has helped me break out of the shell Miss Miller has forced me in. I don't want to go back to that pathetic person. Not with Miss Miller, not with Tricia who seems to want to be the next Miss Miller v2.0.

"I'm going to say this nicely, and ask that you leave me the hell alone, Tricia. I don't work there anymore, I don't work with *you* anymore. Please move on. There are plenty of men who would jump at the chance with what you're offering."

"Mat, please! I don't want anyone else. I only want you, can't you see that? I've loved you since the moment you started in the company. You just never saw me. But you see me now and I'm ready. Take me however you want me. I'll do anything you ask, I promise. You want it up the ass? Take it right here, right now. I don't fucking care who walks by."

I can't handle this shit. I don't want to hurt her but at the same time, I want to fucking strangle her for putting my relationship on the line for her own selfish needs. Fuck!

I still have both of her wrists in my grip. With a last minute decision, I shove her body off me letting her land on her ass on the ground, and slip into the driver's side door, making sure to push the lock button before I start the ignition.

Chapter Twenty-Three

MAT

"You're joking with me right now, right? Tricia?"

"I tell you no fucking lie, Akmal. All these women are going out of their damn minds. I must have a target on me or something." I groan as I lay my head on the back of the couch.

"Damn, I'm glad today was my last day at work. That place is a hot mess. I honestly thought Morty was screwing her."

Both our faces scrunch up in disgust at that visual.

One good thing about the Tricia debacle, is that it gave me the kick in the ass I needed. This whole shit show was set up. I was set up.

How do I fix it? What do I do to get my woman back? Does she even want me back after everything that came out of Miss Miller's mouth?

Sitting on Akmal's couch, I lean forward and put my head in my hands, tugging at my hair as I try to think of a solution.

"Shit, maybe you just need to get your head away from this for a minute. I've got a shoot coming up. It's a car show next week a few cities away from here."

My ears perk up at that. Atsuko might be there, right? "What kind of car show?"

"Another vintage one. And yes, Vero is bringing Atsuko so she can take her mind off things." Akmal's got a smile on his face. They set this up for us. Fuck, this is it. This is my opportunity.

"Fuck yes."

The rest of our talk consists of what we need to bring and the time we need to be there. I need to get Atsuko back, at all costs. She's everything I live for, the only thing I've ever wanted this badly. I can't let meddling people fuck it up for us. Our relationship was never destined to die and be left in ashes.

THE DAY OF THE CAR SHOW STARTS EARLY. AKMAL DIDN'T change any of his equipment or anything, and I guess that last time I came with him, I was late into the shoot as well. It doesn't matter, since I couldn't really sleep that well the night before. All I could think about was seeing her again. I'm nervous and anxious, a weird combination. I want to see her so bad, I really hope Vero was able to drag her out here. *Please let her be there.*

We parked nearby in the designated lot. Akmal is checking the settings on his Nikon.

"Who's the client?"

"A vintage car owner. But he gave me the go ahead to use any of the willing models at the convention around his car."

"Has Vero texted you today, yet?"

Fuck, I feel like a damn schoolboy waiting for news about whether she read my note passed in class.

My eyes are scanning all the car isles and corners for her as we walk towards one of the enclosed buildings, but there's way too much going on to see anyone clearly.

The shoot goes by without a hitch, and Akmal was able to pass more business cards around. He's damn good with his camera. All you can hear is the clicks and rapid shutter speed as he changes position every now and then. A crowd is starting to gather and Pinup girls are lined up to get a picture with the '59 Cadillac. None of them are Vero or Atsuko though, not from what I can see. My mind is wondering where they are, and if any of these car guys are sniffing around them. It makes my blood boil because I know damn well they are. How could they not? She's fucking beautiful.

"Thank you ladies! You've been a great help. I will make sure to send everyone a copy. Please, don't forget to write down your email on this list."

Almost in eerie unison, the ladies around us say, "Yes, Akmal". The giggles are getting on my nerves because I can't hear Vero's or Atsuko's voices if they're nearby.

"The fuck?" Shit, Vero was here this whole time? "¿Qué carajo tu putas creen estas haciendo? What the fuck do you bitches think you're doing? Alright chicas move along!"

Being taller than most of the crowd, I turn towards the voice to see Atsuko looking drop fucking dead gorgeous. My gut is churning at the thought of all the guys she walked by, looking like that. I'm almost snarling at the thought of them getting a whiff of her beautiful scent and following her around.

Her pants are so fucking tight, it's showing too much of her delectable ass and hips. The legs of her pants barely reach her calves, leading to what looks like six inch heels. Her top is just as tight, showcasing her tiny waist, only held on by a slip of fabric that crosses and goes around the back of her neck. The front part dipping so low, her cleavage is on show. My head feels tight again, and I think I'm grinding my teeth because I can see our client basically panting like a dog beside her.

I need to reel this anger in because we can't lose customers before we even get them. But I can feel the red haze starting to creep in from the side of my vision.

I push my way through the crowd and they part for me, making an opening straight to my woman. Fuck, she looks even more beautiful than I remember. Her eyes land on mine and so many emotions are flitting through them.

It feels like everything around us disappears as I try to slow down my heart, standing in front of this angel.

"Atsuko..."

Her eyes widen and I swear they're starting to tear up. Fuck!

"Please, just..."

"Just what, Mat? Let you stomp all over my heart again? Because... I.."

I can't stand this shit. I can't stand this canyon between us. I lean into her because I can't help it. It's like our gravities are aligned, pulling us closer and closer together. Her six inch heels put her close to my height today. Stepping out of my comfort zone, I lean in but she turns her head to the side last minute, landing my lips next to her ear. I take whatever I can get. I'm just glad she hasn't run away from me.

My hand comes up to gently hold her neck, pressing her face against mine. I need to feel her against me, I don't care how.

"I'm sorry. I'm sorry for ever making you doubt me. Just please...come back to me." My voice is breaking but I don't fucking care. I just need her to come back to me and make things right again. I can feel and hear her breath hitch. I'm not sure if it's a good thing or bad thing. Fuck, if there's a higher power out there, please let her hear my plea.

Suddenly, she pulls from my grasp, turns and starts to walk away, swaying her hips like I didn't just bare my fucking soul to her. Vero is not with her, which means she's still with Akmal. I can't let Atsuko walk into a crowd without some sort of protection.

I follow her. I stalk her from afar. I stare daggers into any male that even tries to look her way. I just need to wait her out, wait until she comes to her senses and see that we can't be apart anymore. She has to know right? Know that we're too tied together by this point. I'm fucking mated for life...with her.

Following her through the car show crowd, she doesn't slow down. She also doesn't look anywhere but ahead and it makes my chest constrict. When her arms cross over her chest, my hands itch to pull her into my embrace, but I can't. I'm fucking this up. I don't know what I'm doing. She's the only real relationship I've ever had and she's always been out of my league. I've known this. I've fucking known this!

The smell of hard liquor reaches my nose and my senses go on high alert. It's never good in a crowd of beautiful women like this. It's never good with *my* beautiful woman open to attacks. I'm increasing my speed, trying to catch up with her, when I see a male who looks like her fucking ex get to her.

Shit, I'm seeing red.

I run, and start pushing and shoving people out of my way when I have him in my sights. The grunts and complaints fade away into the distance, until my ears hone in on his voice.

"Atsuko, I could fucking eat you right now. Shit baby, my dick misses you." *Fucking hell.*

Everything is a blur again when I end up tackling him to the ground, knocking some bystanders down near us. The crowd opens up quickly around us, and some feminine screams can be heard. My fists are out of my control, the squeeze of his neck between my palms soothing the rage within me. When I start slamming his head against the concrete ground, other hands are pulling at me, only making me do it harder.

My height and weight would make it hard for anyone to remove me when I'm in the zone. And I'm fucking in the zone now.

"She's fucking mine. Mine!" Am I snarling? More hands are pulling at me, but I use my weight to pull right back. I move my head next to his ear to make sure he can hear me clearly over the crowd's roar. "If I ever smell you near her again, you'll regret the day you put a fucking bottle to your lips because you won't have a fucking head left. I will fucking kill you. Atsuko is mine, make sure you remember it."

I don't get to say the rest of what's on my mind, because I'm finally pulled off the fucker in a snarling rage by a few of the bigger men in the crowd. When my vision clears enough, I look around and Atsuko is nowhere in sight. Fuck, I lost her again. I'm howling like a pained wolf inside as my head feels like it's about to explode in frustration and regret. I stomp away outside of the building to get some much needed air before I lose my damn mind.

Chapter Twenty-Four

MAT

Have I gone crazy? I've been following Atsuko to her job and back, just to make sure she makes it okay, of course. I've been camping outside of her apartment, making sure none of her male neighbors take advantage of her.

When she's grocery shopping, I'm about an aisle away, watching every movement she makes, remembering what it feels like to have those delicate arms wrapped around me when she picks up random items to place in her cart. Watching her hips sway seductively in her dress, as she pushes the cart from aisle to aisle. Glaring at all the men who look a little too damn long for my liking.

Akmal had to remind me to shave the other day, because I'm losing track of time with the shit I'm doing. I'm creeping and stalking. I know it. I've gone off the deep end. But there's nothing else for me but her. My mind is fragmented when I come back to Akmal's home, just to pace around like a caged animal thinking of what I might be missing because I'm not there with her. What if some guy is following her home right now? What if one of her stupid neighbors sneak into her window? What if I'm not there in time to save her from something? What if she needs me and I'm not there to make her feel safe?

Akmal convinced me to go out to eat with him since I'm missing meals when I'm left to my own devices. He tells me I need some new scenery. I need to get my mind off my task. The photography business is booming, and I've done all my duties within a few short hours of concentration. It's really because I'm in a hurry to get back to watching Atsuko.

Watching her at the makeup counter. Watching her talk to Vero. Watching her leave her car to walk to her front door. How can she not be suffering from withdrawals like I am? I'm going crazy every waking minute I'm without her.

"Mat! Are you listening to me?"

Shit. I'm not. I've been moving my food around my dish for the past however long we've been sitting here at this table. I can smell how good the food is, but my stomach doesn't really care for it. I don't have an appetite with all the burdens I have on my shoulders right now.

"You've got it bad, man."

I groan and put my head in my hands on the table. He doesn't understand. I don't have it bad. She's the *only thing* I've ever had. The only thing worthy of holding onto. What is my life without her in it?

Akmal finishes his plate, and I manage to get a handful of bites in before we pay our bill, and start walking towards the front door to exit the restaurant. The cool outside air lets me breathe again, knowing I'm that much closer to being able to watch Atsuko once more.

A feminine gasp escapes near me and I hear, "Mat…"

I really don't feel like talking to anyone right now because it will eat up the limited time I have, but I turn around anyway. There, right outside the front doors of the restaurant, is a woman I wish I never met.

Miss Miller is in a red dress, standing stunned, looking at me with eyes full of desire. It makes me full of rage because it's mostly her fault I'm in this damn predicament. The reason I lost half of my fucking soul, living in this hell on earth.

Akmal is quiet near me. He only knows snippets of what I've told him. He really doesn't know the whole story of what went on between Miss Miller and I.

"I've missed you, Mat. You can always come home whenever you want…"

I snap. It must have been the last straw, and I wasn't prepared for the explosion.

"Get it through your thick skull Miss Miller. I was never yours to begin with. You stole something precious from me once and then you dare to do it again. Never again. NEVER AGAIN! Stay the fuck away from me. There was never an us and there will never be an us. You've made me a shell of myself. Stole half of my fucking soul like the she-demon you are. I hope you rot alone in your home with that fact. I'm done with you. Leave me. The fuck. Alone."

I leave her there with her mouth hanging open, because I need to get Atsuko back, and nothing is going to stand in my way.

I can hear Akmal running to catch up behind me as I continue to just stare ahead. We make it back to our vehicle without another word spoken between us.

———

ATSUKO

I shouldn't be here. Vero still talks to Akmal and I couldn't stay away when he feels so close but so far. Sometimes, I just miss him so badly, I pick up tidbits about where he'll be from Vero's phone conversations with Akmal and just follow him a bit. Does that make me crazy? I mean, I'm not stalking him. I just want to know how he's doing without me. Does he miss me as much as I miss him? I know the exact times he logs online to his game chat servers. Vero's been playing online to try and get closer to Akmal, and I use that fact to my advantage.

I followed him once to the gym just to watch him for a short while, but the way his muscles moved under his sweat just made me go out of my mind with want and regret. I stopped following him to the gym, but continued to follow him to other places.

Gosh, what thirty five year old woman follows her previous lover around? I've gone fucking insane. He makes me insane. When he whispered into my ear at the car convention...my heart skipped a beat. I couldn't take it. I couldn't take wanting him that badly and knowing he's the one that holds my broken heart in his hands. He's the only one that could literally kill me.

It sounded too good to be true.

"...Just please come back to me."

I wanted to so badly but it would show him how weak I am, wouldn't it? He would take advantage of that fact and hang it over my head. I can't go through another heartbreak. I'm barely hanging on as it is. When he started beating Alfonso, my soul couldn't help but be drawn to him again, to his darkness, to his sorrow.

But I couldn't put my weakness in front of me like that, especially in that big of a crowd. I was too scared, and like a coward I ran and didn't look back, until Vero texted me to ask where I was.

And now I'm here. Like a creep, spying on him having lunch with Akmal at a restaurant in town. How pathetic am I?

It's not even like I'm sitting in my car from afar discreetly. I miss his smell. I just wanted to be close enough to smell him.

I'm in regular clothes, not in my usual vintage style. My hair is in a messy bun and I have sunglasses on. He wouldn't be able to pick me out from the crowd. Oh, but I was close enough to hear everything he said to that woman who made me believe there was something going on.

My heart was breaking for him. My heart was breaking for us.

I've never heard him speak to a female that way. The passion in which he delivered his speech left no room for error. He made it known that there was never anything between them. Have I been in the wrong this whole time? It doesn't erase the very real hurt I felt that day, the hurt I still feel because I knew he's always been too good to be true.

I felt no sympathy for the woman. A young gentleman came in quickly to swoop her up. Oh, she was a sobbing mess. But she deserved it because *she* left *me* in a sobbing mess. She seemed to know that guy, since she clung to him quickly like they've already been intimate. I think I heard her call him Travis.

My poor Mat. How do we fix this? How do we make it past what life has thrown at us? I'm so embarrassed for even being here to witness what happened, but I'm glad I was anyway. I think it gave me the courage to kick myself in the ass, to do something instead of just following him around like a psychotic ex-girlfriend. Quickly walking back towards my car, my mind starts to formulate a plan. It has to work because there's no other alternative. I can't bear for it to not work.

Chapter Twenty-Five

MAT

I still haven't gone back to my apartment since the Miss Miller debacle. I'm probably wearing out my welcome at Akmal's bachelor pad, but he hasn't said anything to me. We were able to finish up with editing all of the client's photoshoots and send out emails to the appropriate people. Both of us combined are a quick and efficient team, and business really is booming, uplifting both our spirits.

We're gaming tonight with the usual crew. Akmal has two laptops and an extra headphone set. I don't even know what we're playing, but I'm assuming it's an MMORPG when we boot up the game. He's been texting on and off while playing, I'm not even sure how he can concentrate on the games. Who am I to judge? I can barely concentrate on the day to day with thoughts of Atsuko consuming my every waking thought.

Someone messages me and my eyes do a quick glance down on the screen before my concentration goes back to the dungeon we're trying to complete. We have a good number of people on our team tonight, enough to beat it without too many casualties.

Bellanova and I have been speaking sporadically through some of our time gaming together when she joined our small guild a short while back. I think it's a girl, but who knows these days. It's been random pleasantries. Easier for me to do when I'm behind a screen.

I must have been a little drunk one night because I started spewing to her a little bit about my woman troubles. My mind was probably thinking that it wanted another woman's perspective on the matter. I shouldn't have been drinking to that extent at all, knowing what I know about my father and his habits. But it was hard dulling the ache in my chest. The gym has become such a short lived, temporary fix. At least being at Akmal's place means I can stay out of trouble and my hands won't be coated in red.

Bellanova : You should just tell her that it's not over. Tell her what she needs to hear.

Tinfoilhat : how the hell am I supposed to do that? She's avoiding me.

Bellanova : Don't lie to me. I'm sure you haven't kept your distance.

Tinfoilhat : you got me there. I might be creeping a little. It's only because I can't help it. I don't know what to say though.

Bellanova : Tell her the truth. Tell her and make her understand that you're not going anywhere. Maybe she just needs that reassurance that what you guys had is real.

Tinfoilhat : it was fucking real. I'm just not good with words.

Bellanova : So show her a different way. You know her best. What would make her respond?

My character almost gets killed when thoughts of fucking Atsuko come to my mind. My dick twitches and it's practically howling at me for keeping it away from what it wants. Is it really that easy? What if she fucking calls the cops on me? My mind thinks back to the conversation I had with Akmal that fateful day.

"I mean, she's at my place half the week anyway. What difference does it make if she stays the whole week...and just never goes back? I can take her to work, do whatever she wants me to do."

"I guess it really isn't that different. What does Vero think about that? I mean, they're best friends and all."

"She never crossed my mind. Maybe I'll just keep myself between her legs until she can't say no. Eat her out until she doesn't want to go home."

"I mean, that sounds like it could work. I wouldn't know, since I've never done it. But it sounds legit."

Didn't I say I was going to worship her until she decided to stay with me? Will she even be receptive to me at this point? I'm too drunk for this shit right now. I let my character die, and decide to not respawn. Letting Akmal know that I'm done for the night, I go to his spare bedroom and sleep the buzz off before I do something I might regret.

———

THE CONVERSATION FROM LAST NIGHT STILL LINGERS IN my mind. Nothing else from that night is clear, nothing but that damn conversation. I'm sitting here in my car, rubbing the scruff on my face, waiting for Atsuko to come home from work. What the hell is wrong with me? Am I really doing this?

No time to think, because there she is in all her angelic glory, gliding out of her car towards her apartment door.

My instincts kick in and I leave my car, catching up with her path. The males in the hallway see me coming and quickly retreat back into their apartments. Good. I don't want to be distracted from the mission today.

I stay a short distance behind her, waiting just around the shadows of the corner of the hallway that leads to her apartment. This is exactly why she needs someone to watch over her. Look at how easily I'm hiding. When Atsuko puts her key into her doorknob and opens it up, I quickly push myself inside behind her and shut the door with my back to it, locking us both inside.

Her eyes widen as she looks at me. She doesn't say a thing. I've memorized Vero's schedule by now, and I know for a fact Atsuko is alone. My eyes scan her beautiful features, the slope of her delicate neck, and the way her chest is heaving from her breathing getting deeper. The air in the room is starting to become stifling, but it's now or never. I have to man up, and not let my nerves get the best of me, even though I feel like someone just ripped out my intestines and tied it around my throat.

"Atsuko, please, just listen to what I have to say." My voice is barely above a cracked whisper, but I got it out there.

I can see her throat take a swallow and it makes me think of the days when she's had my dick down her throat doing that. Now I'm nervous and horny. Fuck, stick to the mission.

"What do you want, Mat?"

"I want...to explain myself."

"Does this mean there's been things you've been hiding from me that need explaining?"

"No, I mean, maybe? It's not what it looks like, I promise you. Please, believe me."

"Why should I?"

Shit. Shit. Shit.

I'm down on my fucking knees because she's fucking worth it. She's worth any humiliation she wants to put me through. I've been through worse. She's fucking worth everything.

Her eyes widen and I'm not sure if that's a good thing.

"Miss Miller is a nightmare from a past I've let go of. Yes, she was my first. But no, it was never freely given. I was young and naive. Easily manipulated. But I assure you it's over now.

I promise you, I never touched her after you came into my life."

"Mat..."

I start to strip out of my clothes, imagining I'm peeling my skin off so I can bare my soul to her, bare everything to her. I'm down to my damn boxers on my knees in front of her. What the fuck is wrong with me? God, *please let this work.*

"What are you doing?" She looks scared. *No no no.* I need her to stay on the same page with me, not skitter away.

"I'm begging you to take me back, Atsuko. I can't live without you. I can't fucking eat or breathe without you. It's been a living hell. I'm no good at this shit. It's only ever been you."

"Mat..I.."

Fuck, she's going to rip my heart right out of my damn chest with these kinds of responses. I sit back on my ankles almost in defeat but I can't fail, not when I've come this far. Might as well jump off that metaphorical cliff now.

"Say you'll take me back. I'll do anything. *Any fucking thing.* My soul has been ripped in two since the day you walked out of my life."

She gasps and my eyes lift from the floor to her face. I don't know what she's thinking. I don't know what that look means. All of this is out of my league, but I have nothing else to lose. I've already lost everything important to me.

She slowly puts her bag down onto the couch and says my name, while she makes her finger do the come hither motion.

Is this it? Did I do it right? Am I being a good boy? My dick is telling me to follow the command we're being given.

I'm crawling towards her on my knees when she cradles my face between her hands, the way she used to do. My eyes close, because I'm truly terrified at what she might say to me. I'm afraid to watch her eviscerate what's left of me.

When her lips kiss each of my eyelids, it feels like a kick to the damn chest. How can such a soft small touch affect me like this. Is this good? Does this mean I'm doing good? She's not saying anything.

When her lips touch mine, I explode into action. I don't know what comes over me as I devour her mouth like a man on the verge of death, about to get his last wish before he's sent to the electric chair. The most amazing thing? She responds with just as much fervor.

I'm on my feet now and I'm lifting her body in my arms as she wraps her legs around me. The feeling of her surrounding me, settles my fucking soul. I can literally feel the two pieces being soldered back together by fire.

Our mouths haven't stopped their assault on each other as I make my way to her bedroom from memory. Laying her gently down on her sheets, I look into her eyes, searching to see if what I'm assuming is real. This means we're back together, right? Everything is okay between us? I'm afraid to ask it out loud in case it jinxes the moment.

"Mat."

"Yes?"

"I'm going to need you to do something for me." *Anything. Just say it.* "I'm going to need you to prove to me that I can trust you." *This is it, isn't it? My test. The test. Shit, what if I fail?*

"Whatever it takes, Atsuko. I'll do anything you ask of me." *Shit, please let me be able to do anything you ask of me. My heart is pounding out of my damn chest waiting for her response. She's killing me with this pause.*

When the corners of her lips tilt up ever so slightly into a smile, I feel fear and elation all at once. She pulls me into her space by the back of my neck until we're nose to nose.

"I'm going to need you to dominate me." *Fucking hell.*

My hand goes around her delicate neck and squeezes, as my mouth starts to plunder hers, my tongue seeking entrance to what was forbidden from me for so damn long. She moans into my mouth and my hand squeezes even more. When the second moan gets swallowed in our kiss between our breaths, my hand starts to rip her clothes off frantically. I need her like I need the air to breathe. She is my fucking air. I have so much I need to make up for. There's been so much lost time between us.

When she's naked and fully displayed before me, I pin her arms over her head by the wrists, making her magnificent breasts jut out towards me. My mouth waters even before my lips make it to her nipples. My tongue swirls around her dusky areolas, biting and teasing, and sucking each nipple until her whimpers turn into screams. My cock is straining to come out and play, but not yet. No, I need this for me. I need this to reassure me she will always be mine. I need to mark her.

When both of her breasts are glistening and peaked, my hands remove themselves from her wrists slowly, caressing the length of her arms and sides until they reach below her hips. Pushing both of her legs towards her shoulders, I lick her from her back entrance to the hood of her clit. When my tongue gets that first taste of her arousal, my vision becomes tunneled and I start to eat her pussy with abandon. Her lower lips are puffy and weeping, probably crying for me the way my cock's been howling for her. Her half ass pleas and cries for me to stop goes through one ear out the other as I make her cum again and ride the waves of her orgasm on my tongue. I've missed this. I've missed her taste, that's uniquely her. My body heat is starting to rise up, the room smelling of sex.

Thoughts of Miss Miller and fucking Tricia flit through my mind, making me angry with what they put us through. I let Atsuko's leg rest on my shoulders, as my teeth start to bite, and my tongue comes in to soothe the pain I bring to her pussy lips and clit. Each pass of my tongue across the hood stiffens it up, making it easy for me to suck it into my mouth and tease it. Tricia and her stupid propositions. My finger slides into her hot core, thrusting a few times before bringing her wetness down to her ass and entering there. Creating extra friction with the flat of my tongue against her clit, I can feel her wetness increasing down to my fingers, increasing the lubrication for her back entrance. I've never heard her moan like this, it fuels me. When her third climax peaks and dies off, I flip her over onto her stomach and slam my dick home. Fuck, *home*. The self-imposed banishment is finally done, and I can't help but fuck her hard into the mattress with the rage I felt when she left me there in broken pieces.

I don't want to cum like this, though. It's too easy, too quick. Her pussy would easily milk the life out of me if I let her, and there will be other times for that.

Pulling out quickly, I flip her onto her back, making her head hang off the edge of the bed, right before I shove my dick down her throat. My feet are planted on the floor as I roughly thrust into her. Her gags, and inadvertent throat swallowing, almost make me finish my task too quickly. I play with her nipples that are once again jutting out towards the ceiling, and start to pinch and pluck, the way I've seen her do to herself. Her whimpers and screams around my cock make me groan and slam my fucking balls into her face even more. She never complains, she never pushes me away.

Is this what she's been waiting for all this time? Was this the key to keeping her?

Memories of her telling me to fuck her face come back to me and I do just that. I fuck her like I'm pissed, because I am, but not with her, but the situation with Miss Miller and the fact that Atsuko wasn't my first when she should have been.

I can feel my sack and abs tightening, I shouldn't be doing it this hard to the girl I fucking love, but this is what she wanted. Slamming into her throat a few more times I let go and let my climax consume me, pumping my cum down her throat. I can see her throat swallowing from this angle, see some of it leaking out of the corner of her mouth and it makes me groan in satisfaction. There's a primal need in me to mark her, make her smell like me. When I no longer feel my dick pulsating, I slowly remove it from her mouth. Her intake of air makes me feel good that I was almost able to choke her the way she wanted to be. I'm only doing what she's asking of me.

"Oh my fucking god."

Dropping to my knees in front of her, I kiss her just like that, while she's lying there upside down. I can taste my release on her but fuck if it doesn't make me hard for her again. When we're both almost out of breath, I pick her up and rearrange her back on the bed the correct way before spooning behind her, making sure my arms hold her tightly against me in case she changes her mind. I wouldn't be able to survive it if she left me a second time.

Chapter Twenty-Six

MAT

I'm up way too early, the sun is barely cresting the skies through her window. My fears from last night continue to play over and over again. I still don't feel like we've solidified things. She's squirming subtly and scissoring her legs, but I don't think she's awake yet. My hands have already traveled south, rubbing circles on her clit, and rubbing the wetness that has already accumulated. Last night wasn't enough. It was just to get our frustrations out.

Sliding my dick home slowly, she moans into the pillow, and I start moving in and out of her in a sluggish rhythm. My fingers have left her clit and are now traveling to her puckered asshole from behind, right against my shaft penetrating her slick pussy lips. I kiss the delicate slope of her shoulder before me, licking a wet trail over any freckle I catch. I need to fill every hole, make sure she never has a need for anyone else. All she needs is me. I'll be whatever she wants me to be, as long as she stays by my side.

"Mat..."

I miss the sound of my name on her lips like a whisper. Slowly removing myself from her wet pussy, I gradually push into her other hole. She's already relaxed from my previous ministrations with my fingers. Atsuko starts to push her ass back towards me, letting me know how desperately she wants it. The moment the head of my cock breaches her back entrance, is the moment I let out a sigh.

What was once slow is now starting to become a frantic and brutal pace, a chase to the finish line. If the sounds she's making with her mouth is anything to go by, she loves getting it this hard from behind as well. My hands grab her hips roughly so I can get better leverage to pull her back against me, as my hips continue to surge forward and soon enough, my dick is shooting all of its load into her. We stay connected like that for a long moment, my hands caressing the beautiful curve of her spine, before she peeks at me over that delicate shoulder of hers with a small shy smile.

We both stumble out of bed, and head to the shower to clean up. The room becomes steamy for more reasons than one, as our hands discover each other all over again with the added lubrication of water sliding between our skin.

We shower each other until the water runs cold.

———

Putting on some boxers I must have left at her place, I quietly watch Atsuko sitting across her breakfast table from me, dressed in my shirt. We're eating breakfast in no rush, as we just stare at each other without a word being spoken.

What is going on in her mind? Has she decided to take me back? That's what this is, right? Getting back together? I can't describe what we did together other than explosive makeup sex. But my fear of saying the wrong thing to break this spell is keeping me slowly crunching on this cereal.

Her eyes become hooded and my dick starts to respond, but I still don't say anything. I've taken that first leap of faith and jumped over that metaphorical cliff. The ball is now in her court now with how she wants to play this.

She's eating a small bowl of cereal as well. I've never seen a woman look so fucking desirable eating a damn bowl of cereal, in a wrinkled shirt, with her hair going every which way. But here she is, in the flesh. Fuck, she's real and she's mine...right? She *is* mine. I'm going to make sure she knows it every day so she never doubts me ever again. How do I do that? What do guys usually do in these situations? I can't call Akmal, he's still a damn virgin and can barely hold himself together when he's around Vero.

How does one legally mark a woman as his? My synapses start firing on over time when I come up with the perfect solution.

Taking one last bite, I get up to grab her empty bowl, and go wash the dishes. She startles me a moment when her arms come across my abs from behind in an embrace. Her warmth suffuses confidence in me. This is exactly why I need her.

Once the dishes are done and I dry my hands, I turn around to hug her back. Without her sexy shoes on, Atsuko only stands to my chest, which is perfect for me. My nose grazes the top of her hair, letting me inhale the floral scent of her shampoo. Taking another deep inhale, I mumble into it.

"Atsuko, move in with me."

She lifts her head from my chest and stares directly into my eyes. There's a pause, my heart is jumping, but I need to listen intently to her response.

"You're asking me to move in...with my boyfriend?" Yes, that's exactly it. And fuck yes, that means we're definitely back together.

"Yes. I want to wake up to your scent, I want to go to sleep holding onto the girl of my dreams in my arms. I can't stand being apart from you, it was a living hell that I don't want to visit ever again."

She tucks her head back into my chest, and I don't know what that means.

I can feel her soft lips against my skin when she says, "I'd love to." She's going to kill me with these long drawn out silent moments.

My heart lets out a sigh of relief and then starts jumping again, because I forgot I haven't been home in a really long time and it probably smells like something died there.

Chapter Twenty-Seven

ATSUKO

This place was not as I remembered it. It literally looked like someone died, and it's been left to rot. There's dust everywhere and it looks a bit ransacked, like someone left in a hurry. *My poor baby.*

But having stalked Mat, I know he's been staying at Akmal's place, which probably was the best for him to maintain his sanity. Because I would definitely go insane living in this alone. We both cleaned up what we could, but it was such a slow and go. The job was much bigger than we anticipated, and in the end, had to call in reinforcements: Vero and Akmal. Akmal also has a huge family full of sisters, who knew? They came in after him like a tidal wave, sweeping and cleaning up everything like a super maid service.

They all seem to know and love Mat like a brother. It was nice seeing it, especially after Mat and I started bonding even more over talk of our past, while we were cleaning together.

My heart goes out for his parents and for the fact that he's never returned to the reservation to see his grandparents. I can't even imagine what that would be like. He must have felt so alone. I'm really glad he ended up with a friend like Akmal. What about his grandparents though? Have they ever reached out to him, I wonder? Maybe I can help change that.

Akmal's sisters left hours ago, and as a 're-homecoming' gift of sorts, Akmal got Mat a new computer so that he would have one fully dedicated for work only. That was very nice of him. Vero has work in the morning, so she kisses me goodbye on the lips. She whispers in my ear that she's so happy to see me happy again, and my heart swells. This is why she's my BFF.

When she walks towards the door, I see the boys with wide eyes looking between us and stifle a laugh. That's right, they don't know how close we are.

"Akmal, are you coming or what? Three's a crowd, baby boy."

"Alright."

When they both leave, I grab some drinks for us as we set up a video game for tonight. Mat actually looks really excited to share this with me, he's so damn cute. We're sitting on the floor with our backs to the couch, laptops on our thighs. The game starts to load and our characters are dropped in.

Bellanova : So how did it go?

Tinfoilhat : I've never been happier. I got my woman back.

Bellanova : I knew you could do it.

Tinfoilhat : I just wanted to thank you for pushing me. Shit, and for the alcohol making me tipsy enough to tell you about the crap in the first place.

Bellanova : you are too cute.

Tinfoilhat : LOL. Look, I'm going to be really blunt here. I'm going to have to ask you to refrain from saying stuff like that even if it's through chat. I am happily in love with my woman. I don't want anything to mess up what I worked so hard to get back.

My heart stops for a second in my chest. I turn to look over at Mat who looks like he has the most severe expression on his face. So serious. He's lifting his beer to his mouth when my heart makes me blurt out, "You love me?"

Mat chokes and almost spits out his drink towards his laptop. I slap him on the back a few times and grab him a towel since the drink dribbled down the front of his shirt instead. I'm peppering kisses on the side of his face, as he continues to blot his wet stain. This man of mine.

"What? Where did that come from?"

I smile and try my best to stifle the giggle that wants to come out. Does it make me a bad person? I don't care, I have my man back.

I whisper into his ear, "You are too cute."

The look on his face is priceless. I can literally see the cogwheels clicking slowly, like they're rusted, and then faster like they just got oiled.

"Wait..."

I grab his face before he can ask anything else, and plant a kiss on his lips. Pulling away only slightly, so our lips are still barely touching, I whisper, "I love you too."

He slams his lips back on mine and devours my mouth until I'm breathless. The laptops having been scattered somewhere, we end up sprawled on the ground with Mat on top of me. His hard chest rubs against my breasts, making my nipples tingle, since I don't have a bra on. My legs automatically wrap around his waist, a comfort position I'm coming to find. I almost forgot what I had asked him when his lips travel across my cheeks and to the shell of my left ear.

"You've had my heart in your hands from the first day I met you. I love you Atsuko, don't you ever doubt that."

He made sure I never doubted it again, right there, on the floor of his apartment.

Chapter Twenty-Eight

ATSUKO

Vero and I are starting to pack some boxes for my move into Mat's place. I feel bittersweet about it, because I love Vero. She's my girl.

"How are things going with you and Akmal?"

"Girl, that boy is like a one way mirror sometimes. He does not understand flirting whatsoever. I bet if I was butt naked and bending over, he'd be so polite as to get a sheet to help cover me in case I lost my clothes somewhere. I almost wonder if he's asexual, but I mean look at the cutie. He can't be, can he?"

We both laugh out loud at that, because it's beyond true. Mat is only halfway as bad, but Akmal is a whole different breed. It must be because he's Malay, they have a whole different set of rules, I'm assuming. But I've seen the way he looks at Vero when she's not looking. He's definitely interested.

We pack up half of my stuff and start labeling the boxes. This is going to be a process, but that's okay because this is a step Mat and I need to take. We're both too addicted to each other, too afraid of outside forces coming in between us again. We place the boxes in the trunk of my Camry. Vero steps into the front passenger seat and I start the ignition.

Mat's neighborhood is nice and quiet, right by a cozy little park. No frat boys like our side - I mean, Vero's side. I do worry about her being alone, though. What if she needs help, who will be there for her if she doesn't get to her phone on time?

We're already moving some of the boxes out of the trunk when I tell myself that Vero is a full grown woman, who grew up in the same neighborhood I did. She's got this. I have to trust that she's got this, or else my mind would go nuts with worry over her.

A young blond almost runs into Vero and the big box in her arms. "Yow, watch where you're going chica, I almost dropped this stuff."

"Oh, I'm sorry." She's looking between Vero and I with some sharp eyes. There's something I don't like about her already, and I don't even know who she is. "It looks like you guys are moving in? I didn't know there was an empty apartment on this floor?"

"This foxy mama behind me is moving in with her man, because he can't get enough of what she does to him." This girl. I would slap her ass if my arms weren't holding a big box myself. Vero turns to me and winks before she continues to walk, and I follow right behind her to insert the key to Mat's door.

"I'm sorry, are you sure you have the right door?" What is up with this girl? I have the damn key, right here.

"What's your name again? I don't think I caught it on the way in."

"Oh, uh, Emily. I live a couple doors down."

"Ah.. well nice to meet you Emily. I'm Atsuko. If you don't mind, I need to hurry and put my stuff away, so I can be ready to fuck Mat's brains out when he gets home from work. My man's got a strong appetite, you see."

Vero is laughing at this point as she follows me inside. Emily's jaw is still on the floor.

"Shit, you got that right. That's why I had to kick her ass out. They were keeping me up all night."

We slam the door on her face and continue to place the boxes in their designated areas, before heading back out for the rest of the boxes in the trunk.

"Damn girl, you got your hands full with that one. I mean, I think the problem is that he doesn't know how good he looks, you know? It also makes him damn endearing. Take Akmal for instance, did you see that crowd of girls at the car show? I thought I was about to take off my stilettos and earrings for that shit. It's a good thing he's fucking oblivious and innocent."

I'm grunting and laughing because my arms are sore, but we have one more set of boxes to bring in. Vero is crazy over

Akmal. I have no idea how this shit is going to work because that boy literally has a neon sign over his head that says 'virgin'. Every girl around him can see it, and every girl around him wants to be the one to corrupt his innocence. Him being so damn friendly doesn't help his case whatsoever, it only makes them chase him harder.

I pity the girl who stands in Vero's way, because that broad can be a stubborn and vicious one when she has her sights set on something. And she really wants him.

We're laughing about Vero's failed flirting attempts with Akmal on the way to the car and back when I get a chill down my spine. Before we even get the chance to close the front door, someone shoves us inside.

I drop the box in my hands and I hear Vero do the same before she cusses under her breath.

Alfonso is standing there like a madman, and he smells very strongly of hard liquor with fading bruises on his face. This isn't good. I've since blocked his number when I went on that date with Mat the first time. I've been living blissfully without his drama. How did he know where to find me?

"Atsuko, you fucking bitch. How could you cheat on me?" *What the hell?*

"Get your head out of your ass Alfonso. You guys are NOT together."

"Bitch, you don't think I know it's YOU who's been keeping my girl from me! I know you fuck her and talk behind my back. You're the meddling cunt that made her break up with me. It's always you, Vero!"

I scream when Alfonso throws a punch right at Vero's face, knocking her to the ground. What the hell is happening?

Grabbing the closest thing I can get my hands on, I throw a lamp at Alfonso's head before turning around and running. But he's faster than me for some reason, even though he's drunk. My body hits the carpeted flooring when he tackles me, sending pain up my elbows. Turning my body around, I'm kicking and screaming, throwing punches where I can and scratching his face. But he's got more weight on me, easily subduing me after he comes to his senses from the wound I put on his face. I can feel the bulge between his legs pressing against me. He loves the fight I'm putting up, it's turning him on and it's freaking me the fuck out.

I scream bloody murder and turn my face left and right when he tries to come in for a kiss. He has my wrists pinned down on either side of my head but my legs are still kicking like a she demon. This is not happening right now! I won't let it! I think I knee him in the balls, but it must be his drunken state because it doesn't deter him like I think it would. One of his hands starts tugging on my shirt and my mind is telling me this is it. He's going to rape me right here on the floor.

The door slams open with a loud bang when I scream again, and suddenly, Alfonso's body is lifted off me right before I start to sob. This asshole! How did it come to this? Shit, where's Vero?

I'm turning and crawling around looking for her, when I see Akmal by her side, cradling her as she rubs her face into his chest.

The sound of flesh hitting flesh, and a growl I've come to recognize, makes me get to my feet and turn around just in time to see Mat turning into a beast intent on murdering Alfonso. I'm not sure if I should stop him, or let him proceed with his plans. Alfonso has been a thorn on my side, this was bound to happen. Was it my fault? Did I let it go so far that he would choose this path? A glint of something metal and Alfonso is landing cuts on Mat with a pocketknife. Oh no!

Mat continues like there aren't bleeding streaks of red in random locations. I can't take my eyes away from them. Watching Mat's muscles reminds me of a predator taking down it's kill. The skill and dance to his body's movements are magnificent. Something only found in nature, but before I can get lost in this ballet, my mind slaps me back to reality with the fact that if Mat kills Alfonso, he would be sent to jail.

There's blood spurting from Alfonso's nose and cheek before I decide to run towards Mat and grab his bicep. When he turns, the look on his face is feral. A wild animal operating on instincts, performing what it does best. Mat has a darkness in him that he has to try hard to restrain. Especially knowing what I know now, I need to stop him before he does something he will regret.

"Mat, baby, he's not fighting back. It's done. Come back to me." His arm and shoulder is still vibrating with energy, just barely restrained from the momentum of another swing. I take the risk of cradling his face in my hands, and staring into the eyes of a natural born predator.

"Come back to me."

I kiss his snarling lips and it takes a while before he drops Alfonso's unconscious body like a heap of trash onto the floor. He's shaking throughout the kiss, and his arms are hugging me a little too tightly but I understand his fears. I was afraid too. It was a close call.

"That fucking asshole! I knew he was off his fucking rocker. You should have fucking killed him Mat!" Vero is going ballistic, about to jump at his unconscious body and kick the shit out of him if it wasn't for Akmal holding her back firmly. She's right though. She's always right. I should have never led him on that long.

"I'm so sorry, Mat." My eyes are tearing up with everything that's happened. It's Mat who starts to caress my cheeks with his palms, lovingly placing his forehead on mine, breathing me in the same way I'm breathing him in.

"Never be sorry, Atsuko. I'm more than willing to leave a trail of dead bodies for you, but it would keep me away from the woman I love. Thank you for stopping me, because... I wouldn't have stopped."

My lips crash onto his as his arms come around my waist and lift me up. I can hear Vero talking on the phone, while my tongue seeks reaffirmation from Mat's mouth, about everything that's happened today.

"Yeah, fuck, I want to report a break in and attempted rape. I'm pretty sure this fucker is on probation too."

Chapter Twenty-Nine

MAT

The police removed that piece of trash from our home. I need to call in a carpet service to replace the blood-stained ones in our living room. This is exactly why I need to have Atsuko near me. It reminds me that Vero is still very much on her own, next to those drunken frat boys.

"Vero, are you going to be alright living on your own next to those rowdy frat boys?"

"Wait, you live next to a bunch of drunken college men?"

"Yeah. It's not like you ever asked. Plus they usually stay on their side and I stay on mine."

Akmal looks aggravated, but schools his expression pretty quickly. I feel you man. I felt the same way about my girl.

"You're not living there anymore. What if some other lunatic comes in and none of us are around? We were just lucky that we wrapped up work quickly and came back to see you guys.

Nah, you're coming to stay with me Vero. I have an extra room. It's safer."

"Oh, is that so? Extra room, huh? I do need you to nurse my injury. Would you be my male nurse, Akmal?" I don't know how their relationship can even work with Akmal's culture cockblocking them. In fact, I don't even think he's supposed to have a female in the same house if they're not married.

After clearing his throat, Akmal looks a little uneasy. "Yes. It's a temporary solution but I'm not having you go back to live around a bunch of drunken men. What kind of guy would that make me?"

"Oh, I'd love to find out, Akmal."

"I'm telling you right now, what kind of man I am. You're *not* going back, you're staying with me."

Atsuko and I remain quiet as we watch the show in front of us. It's like watching a tidal wave hit sand. These two are polar opposites.

I rub my nose into Atsuko's hair, making her bring her attention back to me. "Did you get everything you needed from the apartment?"

"I still have a few more boxes to pack up."

"I'll go with you. We might as well bring these two along in case Akmal rethinks his temporary solution. I don't think his family would approve of his suggestion if they ever found out."

"I figured. Not many people approve of Vero, she can be a bit much."

<hr>

THE REST OF THE MOVE WENT QUICKLY. SEEING THE proof of all the males around Vero helped to solidify Akmal's decision. Good. He needs to grab onto her if he's serious about her. Maybe I should take my own advice. Would moving in be enough? Is it enough to make her understand she's mine in all ways? I put a GPS tracker on her phone when she wasn't looking. I need to know where she is at all times, in case I do need to handle something with Akmal and the business.

Akmal and Vero left not too long after dinner before the sun went down. Atsuko and I are lying on the couch, her on top of me, watching mindless television. Dinner was an amazing affair. Who knew home cooked meals tasted so different from ones that comes in a box? Is this what I have to look forward to each day? *I'm a lucky bastard.* Atsuko was most kind enough to be my nurse for some of my superficial wounds. I didn't even feel them when I was pummelling her ex. All I could think about was removing the threat to my female.

My hands are running over her amazing ass covered by one of my shirts, grinding her pussy into my growing erection. She hums against my chest but doesn't reciprocate. It kind of makes me hornier that she's trying to avoid me.

Lifting her up higher, I bring her shirt up and place one of her breasts in my mouth. She stops avoiding me now as her hands run through my hair, light moans escaping her breath. She pushes off me to toss her shirt aside and my eyes are glued to the junction of her thighs. She wasn't wearing panties this entire fucking time. Without having to prompt her, she crawls up my body, and sits over my face. Damn this woman. Happily licking what's offered to me, she starts to grind her pussy into my face more and more. My hands squeeze her ass, forcing her to sit on my face even more as my tongue continues to spear her wet pussy. When her orgasm comes crashing, she cries out in pleasure, and slowly slides back down my body until her face is between my own legs. I've never had a woman worship my dick like she does, and it's the most intoxicating thing. What's even more intoxicating is the fact that she loves the way I dominate her in this position. She makes me confident in myself, the exact opposite of what any other woman has made me feel.

When her mouth swallows my dick, I grab the back of her hair and start thrusting slowly until I can't anymore. When she moans, I can feel the vibration all the way down to my fucking sack and it tips me over the edge, making me climax into her mouth. The feeling of her greedily sucking my cock makes me growl, but she loves it. I hope she never plans to leave me again because this is fucking heaven.

When she crawls back up, I take her mouth in mine, while my slow brain finally comes to the conclusion of what I need to do. I'm lost and drunk in her mouth making love to mine, our tongues tasting each other. When I pull back to catch my breath, I whisper against her lips, "Marry me."

There's a pause between us and she doesn't answer. I kiss her again to further convince her, in case she even considered saying no to me.

Flipping her onto her back on the couch, I dive between her legs and use all the skills I have to make her give me the answer I want to hear. Shit, what if I'm moving too fast? What if she says no? I shove my tongue deeply inside of her, tasting everything she has to give. Her legs start to close in around my ears when I almost miss it.

"Yes, Mat. Oh my fucking god. I'll marry you. Shit, don't stop."

Doubling my efforts and using my fingers to thrust into her, I listen to her scream in ecstasy as I bring her to another climax.

Epilogue

ATSUKO

It took a bit, but with the help of Akmal and his computer skills in addition to my snooping around Mat's stuff when he's not home, we were able to track down his grandparents. They are still living on the Blackfoot reservation in Montana.

It's been a really long time since he's contacted them, and after talking to them on the phone, I found out why. Mat had only just opened up about what happened with his parents, but he never told me he was banished. I never knew he carried all this guilt and weight on his shoulders. He's only mentioned his grandparents briefly during conversations, but I could tell that he missed them, and I'm sure they're wondering how he's doing as well. He's family after all.

I couldn't arrange a visit to the reservation knowing what I know now, so I had to ask them to come and visit us. I hope they're well enough. My mind keeps imagining this poor decrepit old couple trying to drive across a few state lines. I could have asked Mat to do a road trip with me to meet them halfway, but he would be suspicious and I'm not sure how he would receive me going behind his back about this.

My gut tells me I'm doing the right thing. I really *hope* I'm doing the right thing. Mat shouldn't have to be alone without family.

They called about five hours ago during one of their pit stops. I'm getting kind of nervous. I've been busy in the kitchen, making all sorts of meals, even though I don't even know what kind of stuff they like. The whole apartment smells like a restaurant at this point. It's probably going to seep into all the curtains and furniture.

Akmal texted and told me he would try to hold Mat over with work until it was close to time. Looking at the clock over the stove, it looks like he should be home soon. I might have a little time on my hands.

The sound of a key being inserted into the doorknob makes me snap my head that way. He wasn't scheduled back for another thirty minutes.

"Hey, beautiful. Wow, it smells amazing. What's all this? Am I missing an important date for something?"

Greeting him with a hug and kiss on my tip toes, I watch as Mat's face lights into a smile. He really is handsome when he smiles, though every time I try to take a selfie with him, he never does.

Closing the door and locking it behind him, Mat walks me backward with his arms still around me and continues to rain kisses on my face, making me giggle, when there's a knock at the door. *Oh my goodness, this is it. I think it's them. Stay calm, stay calm.*

"Are you expecting someone?" Uh oh, he doesn't look happy. Oh man, I hope I did the right thing.

When Mat opens the door, he stands stock still. I'm getting more nervous by the second when no one says anything. Is it someone else at the door?

"Na-ahks'. What are you doing here?" My heart is swelling even though I don't recognize the first word he said. But it must be them, surely.

"Matunaagd." I can't tell if they sound happy or sad. Even on the phone, Mat's grandparents sounded the same. Mat's body is moving. It looks like they're shaking hands. That's a good sign, right?

"Come in, come in. You must have had a long journey. How did you know where to find me?" Is his voice croaking with emotion too? My poor baby. He's been missing his grandparents even though he doesn't say it out loud.

When Mat turns his broad shoulder to give them room to enter, I see two very sturdy looking elderly individuals step in. His grandmother has a full head of white hair braided back and has the friendliest smile on her face. His grandfather's hair is peppered and tied back, his face clean-shaven with a smile that makes his eyes crinkle in the cutest of ways. I can see a lot of Mat's features in him, they must be his grandparents from his father's side to have genes that strong.

My eyes tear up for his reunion, and I give them both big hugs and usher them to the table where the meals are spread out, waiting to be consumed.

As his grandparents sit down, Mat comes up behind me with a big hug, putting his face close to my ear.

"Did you do this?" I nod my head and turn to hug him back, tightly.

"Thank you Atsuko. This means so much to me."

"Anything for you." Releasing him before I can tear up, I turn to Mat's grandparents with a big welcoming smile.

"So who's hungry?"

———

"You guys are what?!"

"We're engaged!"

"Holy shitballs!" Vero and I are screaming at the news. It's been a few days since Mat's grandparent's departure, and Mat is currently over at Akmal's place for another couple of hours to work on a small family portrait session they recently had.

"Ugh! I'm so jealous of you, Atsuko! But you fucking deserve it. He's great for you. You guys are great together. Now if only I can just get Akmal to even look at me." She's so dramatic. That boy is definitely interested in her. I saw the way he was bristling when he was around the frat boys near her apartment.

"You're crazy, Akmal looks at you all the time when he thinks you're not."

"That is fucking nuts because I have tried to get him to come to my room in so many ways without success. I'm even walking around in a tank and panties all over his place. That boy is a damn saint! It makes me so fucking horny!" She says panties but for all I know she's walking around in a damn thong in front of that poor guy. I really am surprised he hasn't jumped her by now.

"You have your toys, right?"

"I do! But it's not the same!" Vero is utterly whining by this point. I've never seen her this frustrated. But she usually can pick up a quickie at work, I wonder if she still is?

"Are you getting anything at work? You know, to relieve your stress?"

"Atsuko! I can't do that to Akmal. I don't want him to see me that way. I haven't had dick since I started chasing that fucker. And he's making it so hard for me, my pussy is in tears and weeping every time he's around me!" She's groaning as she lays her head back on the armrest of the couch. Poor thing. She's already playing with her tits as we speak. She's so damn frustrated.

Any other time, I would have helped her but now that Mat and I are getting married, I don't think he would be able to handle it. He's a pretty possessive guy, something I love about him. The conversation we had about my relationship with Vero was an interesting one, to say the least. My pussy throbs just thinking about it.

"So...you and Vero?"

We're sitting on the floor in the apartment again. He looks a little scared, like Vero might be competition. It's interesting that I find Mat's jealousy and possessiveness quite endearing versus Alfonso's.

Is this what love does to you? Makes you see everything in a whole new light?

"Me and Vero? We're best friends and yes, we do help each other scratch itches sometimes. But I haven't had an itch since you came into my life. You more than satisfy all my needs."

"...so she's tasted your pussy?"

I can feel my eyes becoming hooded, because Mat is trying to get at something. I just know it. Whatever it is, the low timbre of his voice is turning me on right now.

His hands peel back my cotton shorts quickly, removing the panties with them making me gasp. He's become more and more aggressive since we've been together.

I love it.

His lips touch my inner thigh and my legs fall open to make room for his broad shoulders.

"You know this pussy is mine, right? No more girl time down here. I'm not going to tell you again."

My breath hitches because it sounds like a damn challenge. I can't help but rise up to his bait.

"Why's that? What happens when I'm a bad girl?" *Why is my voice so breathy right now? I moan when Mat uses the flat of his tongue to lick my swollen lips all the way up to the hood of my clit, sucking it into his lips, while he stares at me with his dark eyes.*

A few more sucks and a few more licks, Mat undresses quickly before finishing me, leaving me a hot and bothered mess. His dick is hard and angry looking, and it's pointing right at me accusingly. The precum glistening against his piercing and head is making my mouth water. But the look on Mat's face says he has something in store for me.

He crawls between my legs and pushes my chest down until I'm on my back. His hand is going towards his cock.

Thwack thwack!

Oh. My. God.

Thwack!

Mat dick slaps me hard, making my hips jump right before he leans in and starts to rub his shaft against my wet labia folds, poking the head of his cock against my clit. I'm breathing heavily, and my mind is still reeling over the fact that Mat dick slapped me when I feel him bite into the crook of my neck right before he slams home inside of me.

"Sorry babe, I can't help you. And I'm going to have to ask you to refrain from touching yourself around here. Don't pull me into that! I'm engaged with Mat!"

She's pinching her nipples through her shirt a few more times before she groans and stops her ministrations.

"Fuck, you're right. I'll stop. I'll stop."

Her eyes are closed and suddenly she pops up into sitting, scaring the shit out of me. "What if I get him drunk and blow his mind? He wouldn't be able to say no to me then, right?"

I'm laughing. This girl. "How do you come up with this stuff?"

"It's not me! It's my pussy! She's telling me what to do. She's lonely, and she wants Akmal badly. He has got to be the most off limits man I've ever met. It only makes me want him more!" This poor girl. She is suffering. I don't know how to help her.

The door opens, surprising us. The boys are home early.

"Hey beautiful. We finished early and wanted to get back. Did you two have fun?"

"Yeah, I'm glad you're here." I jump into his arms and he catches me with ease. Our welcome home kiss is starting to get a little heated and I can hear Vero groaning behind us. Oops.

"Sorry, Vero." What kind of a friend am I? Vero literally has the female version of blue balls as we speak.

"It's alright Chica. Come on Akmal, let's go home."

"Er...Yeah, we'll catch you guys later."

———

AKMAL

This woman drives me nuts. My dick is going to stain every single pair of pants I own. My culture dictates that I can't even whack off. How can a woman be this damn sexy? I'm trying my best to remain calm and polite, but it's getting harder and harder the more I'm around her. Ironic because it's not the only thing getting harder the more I'm around her. Feels like my dick is going to fall off with how stiff it's been without any relief.

When I drive her home, I think of the fact that I probably shouldn't even be doing this. What if my family finds out? Shit, what if one of my sisters decides to come by? But I couldn't leave her at her apartment all alone, basically surrounded by a bunch of men who would jump at the chance to be with her. I want a chance at her before anyone else. I saw her first.

How do I fix this? How do I fix this and not go against my culture? There's really only one way I can touch her, but I don't know if I should. She'll probably think I'm crazy.

My thoughts are running a mile a minute as we get out of the car and start walking toward our door. *Our.* We're basically together, aren't we? Isn't this how the regular folk do it? Damn, the way her ass sways when she walks in front of me is hypnotizing. I don't say any of these things because I'm trying to be a damn gentleman, but it's getting really difficult.

"Akmal, do you want to watch a movie with me?" *I want to do so much with you, if only you knew.*

"Yeah, what do you feel like watching?"

"Whatever you want. I'll go grab us some drinks." It's a bit early for drinks but I'll do whatever she wants. She's taking over my every waking thought. Her scent is making me desperate to sit near her. She smells like something light and airy with a hint of sweetness.

We start watching Star Wars Episode 1 and three quarters into the movie, I'm feeling a little drunk. Damn, how many bottles has she handed me? Every time our fingers brush, I feel electricity zap, and it travels right down to my dick. I just wanted to be able to sneak these little touches, again and again, when she thrust the bottles my way. Does that make me pathetic or what?

I must have been fading in and out because I can feel the soft cushions of the couch beneath me. When did I lay my body down? Opening my eyes, the room starts to warp a little. Damn, this isn't good. How the hell am I going to get to my room?

A warm body is on top of me, my slightly drunk addled mind thought it was a blanket for some reason. But blankets don't moan and rub themselves on you, do they? Shit. We shouldn't be doing this. I'm not supposed to be doing this. *She feels so hot between her legs.* It feels like she's rubbing herself on my shin.

"Vero?" My voice is croaking from what she's doing to me, and from me being scared of the position I found myself in.

"Shh...let me take care of you. It looks angry." Wait, what?

Shit shit shit. When did my pants get undone? I can feel her warm breath across my rock hard dick and I'm swallowing a gulp down my throat because I want to push her off and I want to keep her there at the same time. *What do I do? What do I do? Is it getting hotter in here?*

My mind is processing too slowly, because I'm still trying to figure out how I got in this position to begin with, when something hot and wet envelops the head of my dick making me almost jump out of my skin. Holy hell, is this what I've been missing out on? *My god, this can't be real.*

Her tongue. My fucking god, *her tongue.* She's doing some sort of witchcraft down there. I can't take my eyes off her, I'm under her damn spell. The room warps a little bit every now and again, but the sight of Vero's head bobbing up and down on my shaft keeps me somewhat focused. How can something feel this good? If a mouth feels *this* good, what would a pussy feel like? *Shit, stop thinking like that. Control yourself.* The light from the TV is casting fascinating shadows on her face as the credits roll up in my periphery. Trying to think random thoughts still doesn't stop my abs from tensing up with each suck she performs on her way up my shaft.

When her hand starts to fondle my sack, I explode into her mouth with a loud groan and jerk of my hips. Shit, should I have done that? What the hell did I just do? Fuck. But I can't stop. It feels so damn good. That was the biggest orgasm of my damn twenty eight years of life. Which doesn't say much really.

The way her mouth suctions on my cock as it continues to shoot out jets of cum, almost sobers me. Damn, look at how beautiful she is. She loves it, *I think.* I mean, she's moaning on my cock as she does it. It must mean she likes it? My mind is starting to clear and the situation at hand is starting to rear its ugly head at me. We've gone too far. Beyond too far. There's only one way to fix this. But how will she receive it?

Vero gives my dick one last sultry lick right over my slit, making me groan again before she climbs over me and brings her body down flush with mine. I love the way she feels on top of me.

My hands slowly, ever so slowly, touch her cheeks. I'm scared, I've never done this before. This is all so new to me. But if it has to happen, I wouldn't want it with anyone else but Vero. My hands become more confident, and firmly cradle her face in front of me. She's so fucking soft, the most beautiful woman I've ever seen. She's a hurricane that came into my peaceful existence, knocking me to my damn knees. I thought I was strong before I met her, but what just happened between us proved me wrong. She destroys any control I thought I had.

"Hi." Her breathy voice, in combination with her stunning smile, pushes me over the edge. I have to do this.

"Will you be my wife?" It almost feels like my heart doesn't beat again until I see her smile widen even more.

"Damn, if all it took was a blowjob to make you see me, I would have done it sooner. Fuck it. Why not? Hell yea, I'll be your wife."

She kisses me before I can stop her and tell her that we need to refrain from anything else before marriage.

But like she says, fuck it. Just one kiss wouldn't hurt. We're getting married anyway, right?

Author's Note

A beta reader had mentioned wanting more of an interaction between the grandparents and Mat during their reunion. After consulting my person on the traits she noticed in her husband and grandfather who is Blackfoot, I was informed that the men in her life are very stoic. Hands-on attention is not given as freely as some Americans.

So why did the story have to end like *this*? Why not some sort of build-up like with the other two main characters? Or maybe even a dreaded cliffhanger?

The person I was consulting on Akmal's culture informed me that if Vero even thought of leaving the guy hanging, he would probably avoid her like the plague and hide at his parent's house. It was an interesting move I had to make in order for the two side characters to be ABLE to move forward together (and I really wanted them to have a book!).

Another question that was brought up was why would Vero disregard/disrespect Akmal's culture with that move of getting him drunk? My answer is because all those times they "hung out" at lunch were more of Vero talking his head off and the poor guy just nodding his head and smiling in order to be polite. Remember, he is good when it comes to professional conversation, but not when it comes to relationships and girls. He is allowed to date, but no touching of *that sort* until marriage.

Now that the stage is set for a wedding ceremony (Akmal's mother is probably already setting it up before Vero even gets there) can you imagine loud mouth, overconfident Vero having to restrain her inner self when the wedding happens? I was informed that this would actually be a WHOLE DAY affair. She would have to refrain from cursing as well.

I hope you guys are excited to see what book 2 has in store for us all! These characters take over my story as I write. Even I don't know what's going to happen next!

Playlist

Queen - Bohemian Rhapsody
The Dresden Dolls - Coin Operated Boy
Imelda May - Mayhem
Imelda May - Tribal
Black Label Society - Bleed For Me
Peggy Lee - Fever
Postmodern Jukebox - Seven Nation Army
Christina Aguilera - Trouble
Imelda May - Pulling the Rug
Big Bad Voodoo Daddy - Maddest Kind of Love
Lavay Smith & Her Red Hot Skillet Lickers - Oo Papa Doo
Christina Aguilera - Ain't No Other Man

If you get your kicks in a magical manner, order toys from websites like bad dragon, and prefer your monsters *in* your bed instead of *under* them, then Y. D. is your girl.

Writing everything from spicy dark fantasy to fluffier-than-a-cool-marshmallow romance, Y.D. La Mar has her fingers in all sorts of man-meat pie, and the sky is the limit. Somehow, this magical mistress manages to balance her spicy author life with her responsibilities as a mom, a wife, and a resident of Sin City—*oh, irony, you've felled me.*

When the world is full of black-and-white, Y.D. plays in the grey zones, spending her time creating new ways to shock and awe her editor, as well as her readers.

Follow Me!

Want updates and sneak peeks?

Sign up for my newsletter!

Also by YD La Mar

STREET ARRHYTHMIA TRILOGY

The Scent of Jasmine

For The Love of Import & Blood

To The Beat of The Streets

Spinoff

Arachnophilia

REVERSE HAREM

Warring Suns

SCI FI

The Essence of Esme

PARANORMAL

The Hunger of Thieves

Heart of The Reaper

Heart of the Reaper: Tales from the Underworld

Soul of The Reaper

Fate of The Reaper

Bury Me Alive

Lead Me Through The Fire

PSYCHOLOGICAL THRILLER

The Truth Enslaved

CONTEMPORARY

The Formation of Us

The Conception of Us

The Revelation of Us

The House of Eden (cowrite)

When the Bloom Burns (cowrite)

OMEGAVERSE

Gero

Bernhard

Severin

Dystopian/Post Apocalyptic

We Are the Fallen

MONSTER SHORT STORIES

Sinful Attraction

The Sky Below

Maeonia

Between Heaven and Earth

Fantasies Inflamed

Her 13th Hour

Ignus Fatuus

ANTHOLOGIES

Used and Bound

Captured by Darkness

Until the End

After the Rain

Into The Woods

A Foster Fling

Bound by Monsters

Once Upon a Nightmare

Monsters in Love: Lost in the Dark

Monsters in Love: Lost in the Forest

Monsters in Love: Monstrous Ever After

Monsters in Love: Lost in the Deeps

Monsters in Love: Aloha Nui Loa

Pollinators

The Red Key Club: Valentines Day Edition

The Red Key Club: Halloween Edition

Creepy Court

Crimson Vendetta

For the Love of Villains

SHARED WORLDS

Inferno World

Games of the Underworld

Rise of the Dreads

Monsters Ball

Rescue Me: A Hero Romance Collection

The Conception of Us

How did a 28 year old virgin like myself catch a woman
like her?
From the first time I saw her behind the camera lens, I knew
she was out of my league.
Every man's fantasies come to life, I couldn't get her out of
my mind.
Out of all the guys she could have, she chose me, the nerdy
Malay guy.
I'm so nervous about bringing her to meet my family, my
palms are sweating.
What if they're too much for her?
What if I'm not enough for her?
What if she decides she can't handle the fact that we can't do
anything before marriage?

Catching her isn't going to be enough.
The hard part is finding a way to keep her.

Courtesy Warning: This book may contain triggers for
some. Triggers include but not limited to: light BDSM

The Conception of Us Snippet

VERO

"Wait, what. Say that one more time, I don't think I heard your right the first time." I black out my screen when I hear Akmal right next to me. I'm not ready to talk about this yet. I need to find out more information first before I start throwing around false information. Plus there's no point in worrying about something you're not sure of yet.

Straightening up, I smooth down my clothes and look at Akmal who hasn't moved an inch from where he's standing - a foot away from me.

"Yeah, I'll call you back." He's staring at me and I don't know why. I try to give him a smile.

"Is everything okay?"

"Yeah, everything's fine. Did you have a good time with Atsuko today? Do anything interesting?"

"I always have fun with my BFF. We didn't do much, just went to eat at Big Burgers and hung out."

He's staring at me and I'm starting to feel like a mouse under a microscope. What was he and Mat talking about? It had to be Mat, no one else really calls him. All his photography stuff is handled via emails and messenger online.

"Hmmm. You guys eat a good meal then?"

"Yes, it was absolutely delicious as usual. The food went way too fast, they need to make bigger sizes for their combos."

"Is that right?"

Akmal's phone rings again and I watch as he connects it without taking his eyes off me. My hands are starting to get clammy from the tension in this room. Is it getting hot in here?

"Yeah." His eyes are scanning my face, but his expression is still so blank. I'm on pins and needles now. What is going on?

"Thanks for letting me know. I'll call you back." Akmal hangs up and tosses his cell phone onto the couch, the move startling me with how abrupt it is.

"So, nothing else happened today on your date with Atsuko?"

"Not really, we just kind of hung out at her place for a little."

He stares at me, I stare at him. The tension in the room amps up tenfold but I'm not one to back down from a challenge or break first. No no no. We were being good girls. Yup. Mmmhmm.

"Vero."

"Akmal."

"Fucking hell." Wait, what? "Vero, do you need to tell me something?"

"Nooo. Why would I?" Dammit, why am I like this?

"No?"

"Nope." I make the 'p' pop for emphasis because I'm feeling a little extra right now. He needs to get off my back.

"No." He's repeating me but it's coming out like a low whisper. I can tell he's trying to suppress a grin and it's making me try to suppress my grin. Challenge accepted fucker.

But when he takes the last couple of steps towards me with dark hunger in his eyes, I gulp and start to feel like a little chicken. When his scent surrounds me, my eyes flutter a bit and I have to mentally slap myself to stand strong against his sexy ass ways.

What do they say about facing a predator? Don't look away. *Alright Vero, come on girl, don't look away.*

We're basically toe to toe. He leans in a little and I inadvertently lean back a little, my ass on the arm of the couch.

His hand shoots out and grabs the back of my neck as he leans in, putting his cheek against mine. "Are you lying to me, Vero?" The octaves of his voice have gone so low I can feel the timber of it down to my core. Oh my god. *Stand your ground!*

"N-no."

He starts kissing the crook of my neck, his facial hair scraping my skin and making it prickle. When his tongue starts to lick and his lips start to suck and nip, my legs get a little weak. He's sucking hard now and it makes my nipples perk up, rubbing against the lace of my bra. The room is getting hotter because I swear I'm sweating between my tits right now from how he has me cornered.

He gives me another hard suck to the point teetering on pain then proceeds to lave at the spot with the flat of his tongue, soothing it away and making me sigh. "Did you go to the store with Atsuko today?" His tongue is trailing up my jaw until he captures my mouth in his, invading it, owning it. He's making my brain foggy. He's playing me like a damn fiddle.

"What does that matter?" I manage to say between our lips colliding. Oh dear lord, Akmal growls into my mouth and starts plundering it with full force, dominating my movements with his. I can only go along for the ride as I find myself lost in what he's doing to me. Our eyes are still open as we stare at each other, the tension in the room so thick you can cut it with a knife.

His hands are moving in quick succession while his mouth continues to ravish mine. Our teeth hitting each other at times from how rough our movements have become. My body is being forced into different positions and the cool air coming between us now and again tells me he's been stripping me like a damn magician.

How he got me naked except for my bra this fast, I have no idea. This man is far from the virgin I remember. He pulls the soft lace cup of my bra down and fists my hair, tilting my head back and taking my nipple into his mouth.

Oh, but he's not in a playing mood today, no. A suck, a lick and a nip later, he grabs my ass and hefts me up. My legs automatically wrap around him to prevent me from falling, trapping his hard cock between us. His head comes forward to take my other nipple in his mouth as he walks us somewhere. With my arms wrapped around his shoulders and my fingers threading through his hair, my mouth is gaping open from how hard he's attacking it. With each step he takes, his shaft rubs against my clit and wet pussy lips, making us glide against each other.

My back hits a wall and it almost knocks the air out of me until Akmal shoves his cock all the way in with one hard stroke.

"Vero -" *Thrust* "Did you" *Thrust* "go to the store today?" *Thrust thrust.*

I'm speechless with how hard he's pounding into me. He's hitting things he hasn't hit before with his enthusiasm. I open my mouth to say something but I can't do anything else but gasp and moan like a wanton ho.

His hands grip my ass even harder with my non answer and Akmal starts to force my hips against him every time he pounds into me.

"You're such a little liar, Vero." My pussy is already fluttering with everything that's happened. "Why do you need to be brat all the time?"

Oh my god. Am I expected to answer that right now? How fucking rude of him to ask! Oh shit, I can feel my body tensing, the sensations are getting higher.

"Is it because you want me to fuck you? Is that it?" Oh fuck, what is he doing with his hips. He's twisting it somehow. Oh dear god.

"Is it because you like to get punished for being a bad little girl?" Yes! Hell yes! But I can't tell him that because..because..

I cry out as one of his twisted grinds hits me in the right spot and I'm seeing fucking stars as my body tightens and almost wants to convulse. My pussy is clenching around his cock and a few more thrusts later - banging my head against the damn wall - Akmal is groaning into my chest, biting me right under my collarbone.

The feeling of his cock spurting cum inside me makes me ride waves after falling off the climax cliff. It's glorious and I'm panting. Akmal pulls us away from the wall and lowers us ungracefully onto the carpeted floor when he just lies on top of me, trying to catch his breath.

My hands are petting him and rubbing his back, the dampness of his skin making my hands stick a bit. Akmal is nuzzling my breasts and kissing it as he sneaks in, "I know what you did, Vero."